Madame Sorel's Lodger

MADAME SOREL'S LODGER

TRACY WISE

ISBN 979-8-9908030-4-6 (paperback)
ISBN 979-8-9908030-5-3 (ebook)

Published by Type Eighteen Books
www.typeeighteenbooks.com

*To Mum and Dad, for the music
of words and painting*

Table of Contents

1 – Blue Shutters

The Artist arrived on the early morning train from Paris and decided to make his way on foot to the town of A–. It was a glorious day, the morning still in full bloom, the temperature not too hot with the right touch of breeze. A day to walk.

The countryside that greeted him was low slung, fresh fields dotted with blossoms amid the green stalks and scattered smudges of trees.

The area was far from fashionable, a farming community only, and spring planting was underway. The only people he passed were in the fields, bent over rows of future wheat or lavender. Orchards of fruit and olive trees intermittently flanked the road. He passed one field filled with grapevines.

Birds twittered in their nests, and the road had retained more morning dew than it would later in the year. This world was all hues of color, a bursting cornucopia of light and promise and birdsong. As days grew warmer, it would become dryer and dustier, but not today. No, not today. Clearing out the smoke and mug and gugg of noise and dirt, and debris of fires of coal and wood that salted and suffocated the city—that was what he wanted to do.

He left the fields and passed through a tiny forest—if it deserved such a name. And then, before he knew it, he was on the lip of a town. He re-checked the directions on the paper in his pocket, which stated, "A– is the first town past the fields and the little forest." One house became several, and then his feet began to hit the occasional cobblestone until he was walking on fully cobblestoned streets.

He passed a solid, well-appointed house on the outer edges of the town, but those further in were narrow and leaned into each other. The central way could barely fit a carriage or cart without hitting the walls of the houses on either side. The gables on some of the structures almost touched, remnants of a medieval past which had been scraped away in other parts of France to accommodate wide boulevards and more modern architecture.

The street abruptly widened for several meters, to welcome an intersection which broke up the straight line of houses. Slightly ahead on the right, he saw the town's café bar, with scrubbed wooden tables in a small courtyard and chairs leaning up against them. He could imagine them filled for the lunch or dinner hour, and his stomach rumbled. But no, first his room.

At that moment, two boys approached. Their furtiveness indicated they were on the run from some type of responsibility, but he interrupted nonetheless.

"Messieurs," he said, "do you know the house of Madame Sorel?"

The formality of the address stopped the boys in their tracks. They were neatly dressed: blue serge suits and clean white shirts. Flat caps covered their dark heads. The shorter one ducked behind the taller, who squinted doubtfully at the Artist. Finally, the taller one spoke. Giving a little bow, he responded, "Monsieur, the house of Madame Sorel is there, on the left, with the blue shutters." He gestured back the way they had come.

"I thank you," the Artist replied. He picked up his valise and painting supplies and continued down the cobblestone way.

"Monsieur—what are those?" the taller boy called out.

He halted and turned to face them again. "Painting supplies. I am an artist."

"An artist," the boys mouthed to each other. Suddenly, they took off running, laughing as they went, and quickly vanished behind the corner of a building.

And then the Artist was there, his destination as suggested to him a couple of months ago from a fellow artist he had met at his favorite café in Paris.

He walked up to the front door of the house with the blue shutters and a room to let. He knocked. No answer. The small town all around him remained silent except for the whispering tickle of a breeze behind his ear, the distant barking of a dog, and the shout which silenced it.

He knocked again.

Silence.

"Madame Sorel." He mouthed the words silently as he stared at the blue shutters, suddenly hesitant to break the stillness.

2 – Madame Sorel

He snapped back to himself as a grumble sounded from deep within the house. This grumble grew louder until it reached the door.

"Half a minute. Do not pound so! I am coming. What time of the morning do you think this is?"

The sound of locks turning, the ponderous opening of the door, and the figure of Madame Sorel—for it could only be she, with the sense of authority she exuded—appeared. The flash of blue in her eyes gave a surprising sense of youth to a face that otherwise showed years of hard work and grim determination. She drew herself up at the sight of the man on her front stoop. Her lovely eyes narrowed, and her mouth set into a thin line.

The would-be lodger swiftly pulled his hat from his head. "Madame Sorel, I am the Artist."

Her gaze swept from crown to toes. "I can see that."

"I wrote to request the availability of a room with board, and I have your reply." He fished in his pocket and located the large, folded paper he had consulted for directions, which he extended to her.

She waved his hand away. "*Oui*, Monsieur. I do recall. You are earlier than I expected, that is all. I thought you would not arrive until the afternoon train. The room is still available, per the terms in the letter. Are these terms acceptable?"

At her response, a wave of relief rolled through his body, and he nearly staggered with a weakness he had been holding at bay.

With an exhale, the world around the Artist came into sharp focus. He saw that Madame Sorel, in addition to the startlingly blue eyes, was possessed of a thick head of dark hair, only slightly streaked with gray, and pulled back into an ample bun. She wore a simply cut, dark gray dress, with ruched lace around the collar, covered by a serviceable apron with handprints of flour still visible just above the pockets. He had been silent too long; the set of her mouth was deepening.

"*Oui*, Madame. They are acceptable."

She *hmphed*, shot him a look that clearly meant "Wait there," and retreated briefly into the house. She returned holding a key set on a single, small iron hoop. He stepped back as she shut the front door and pointed to a staircase running against the exterior of the building's far side.

"The room is up there." She set off in that direction, causing him to stumble backwards into the road, and he followed until he was behind her climbing the stairs.

Madame Sorel's house was the first along the street with a narrow gap between it and its neighbor, leaving just enough room for the staircase and a strangled alley which continued around to the rear of the building. At the top of the stairs, she inserted the key into the lock. Using her weight to push the door open, she entered.

After a moment, the Artist stepped across the threshold into the room. She remained by the open door while he turned slowly, taking in the space. It was small but comfortable. The floor was made of scrubbed wooden planks, and the single bed occupied the far wall directly opposite the door. A quilted counterpane covered the bed; two surprisingly new pillows added a note of comfort. A window, its shutters slightly open to let in the cool morning air, sat above and to the left of the bed's headboard. To the right of the window, a sturdy wooden rack with four knobs for clothes was affixed. He noticed the simple washstand in the far-left corner, with a fresh bar of soap next to the ewer and basin, and the clean cloth hanging to its left. Over the top of the washstand hung a small mirror, so he would not have to rely on imagination to trim his beard. A modest and unadorned wardrobe took up space along the final wall, to his right, and two chairs with straw woven seats sat opposite the wardrobe.

"It is a solid room," his landlady said. "No chinks in the wall to let the winter through. The girl will clean it every morning and do a thorough scrub on Saturdays. I require one week's payment in advance. Rent will be due weekly, on Fridays. You can leave it with me, not with the girl. I can provide a cup of coffee and porridge after first light, and bread and cheese for lunch. If you wish to take lunch with you, that is acceptable. I do not provide dinner. You may arrange with Monsieur Capet, the café owner, for those meals. I run a good house, a respectable home, so there will be no carrying on of any type in this room. Is that clear, Monsieur?"

His eyes were drinking in the room's light as he followed the moving trails of various colors as they danced across the space. His legs felt wobbly, and he concentrated on remaining upright. Her voice appeared to come from far away as he navigated the rush of sensations on top of his fatigue, and it took him a moment to catch up with her final "Monsieur."

"*Non*, I mean, very clear, *merci*, Madame. *Oui*, this is exactly what I need and meets all my expectations. So, you wish the first week now?"

She *hmphed* a yes and stated the sum.

He carefully extracted some coins from his pocket and found himself stupidly staring, unable to count them. With an exasperated "*pffttt*," she reached into his hand to separate the correct amount before gazing at the coins in her own hand and nodding in satisfaction. Before she went out, she handed him the key on its ring.

"Here is your key, Monsieur. I possess another copy of the key in my house. Either the girl or I will always knock and announce ourselves before we enter to take care of the room. You do not need to be present for us to do so."

"That is acceptable, Madame."

"Very well. Please come down to the kitchen in the next hour, and I will provide you with coffee, bread, and cheese to replenish you after your journey." A quick sniff followed the statement, but a glance at her eyes did not indicate any softening.

"I wish you joy, Monsieur, during your time in our village. How long will you stay? You did not mention in your letter."

As long as I possibly can until the money runs out, he thought, but such a statement would be dangerous with this formidable woman. "A few months, Madame. I am not yet sure. It will depend on my paintings and how they come."

She gave him a look which combined skepticism and dismissal, but only nodded and stepped out over the threshold.

"Oh, Madame."

She paused.

"Might you direct me to a nearby carpenter or someone who may assist me with preparing some additional canvases? I would rather not incur the expense of ordering them from Paris. I know how to make them myself, though I do need some assistance."

"Monsieur Philippe," she said, and continued on her way. He heard her voice floating back as she descended the stairs. "Continue in the direction you came and take a right at the house with the red door. His workshop lies beyond."

"*Merci*, Madame."

He closed the door and sank onto the bed, his knees buckling with exhaustion. His eyes focused on one of the wooden chairs, honey-colored with a near-matching yellow straw seat. It looked sturdy. The brightness of the colors lifted his spirits. Good.

He lay back and closed his eyes, careful to keep his muddy shoes off the coverlet. He would rest for a minute and then go down for a cup of coffee and some food.

He was asleep in minutes.

3 – The Kitchen and the Carpenter

He headed down the stairs and through the alley to reach the back of the house, assuming he would find a door to the kitchen there. This door was also painted blue, like the shutters, but it was scratched and worn. He cautiously opened it and peered in.

A plain but comfortable room met his eyes. It had a wooden floor which, like his room upstairs, had been scrubbed over the years until it was practically white. Dishes rested on shelves above a sideboard, and along the wall facing the roughly paved rear courtyard was a large stone sink directly below a long window which provided the main source of light. A golden-haired young woman stood at the sink, scouring dishes and setting them to dry on a nearby rack. He cleared his throat, and she jumped, startled out of whatever dream she was in.

He ducked his head. "*Bonjour*, I am the Artist. I am staying in the room upstairs." He pointed upwards.

She nodded, drying her hands. "*Oui*," she said softly. "Madame told me. She also told me to fix you coffee and bread. Please, sit." She indicated a thick, oak table, anchoring the middle of the room, and then headed towards a cast iron stove taking up the third wall of the kitchen. A coffee pot was warming on the top. She poured coffee into a well-used crockery mug and brought it to him. She darted into a pantry he hadn't noticed before and returned with a hunk of cheese and a loaf of bread wrapped in a cloth. She set both on the table, alongside a plate and knife, and then returned to her work.

The Artist's stomach gave a growl. He used the knife to cut a couple of thick slices, gratefully listening to the crisp crunch of the fresh outer layer of the loaf, and then he carved off a chunk of the cheese. He took his first few bites quickly, but then made himself slow down to chew and savor it. He did not wish to appear a starving man. He carefully took a swallow of the coffee, still piping hot. Once he had eaten, he continued to sit there and close his eyes. The ache in his belly was subsiding.

He opened his eyes to see the young girl staring at him. When her eyes caught his, however, she blushed and returned to her work at the sink. Her eyes were blue, a hue more faded than her mistress's. He could not help but notice the dark circles underneath. Her vulnerability drew a soft pity, and he asked, "What is your name?"

"Gretchen," she replied.

"Gretchen! That is a strange name for a girl from these parts."

She shrugged and turned slightly to face him. "Nonetheless, Monsieur, it is my name. I am a foundling, under the care of Madame Sorel for these many years. Her husband served in the military in Germany. He found me on his way home, or so he claimed. I do not remember. And she named me that. Also, on account of these." She used her free hand to tug at one of the two thick, yellow braids that reached nearly to her waist. "Like a German milkmaid, she says."

"But surely there are French girls with golden hair."

She shrugged again.

"And Monsieur Sorel, is he living?" Really, where was this need to keep talking coming from? She was but the servant girl. Yet there was something—the eyes? the hair?—that drew him to her.

The motion of her arms stopped, and she shook her head. For her, clearly the conversation had come to an end.

After a moment, he stood. "I thank you, Gretchen. I will see you tomorrow morning when I return for my breakfast."

He left the silent kitchen and stepped around the house to the front. Quiet, clean, and serviceable; he could not ask for more. The blue shutters kept their own counsel.

Feeling reassured, he went into the street, still empty except for one young woman hurrying out of the house opposite towards the café. As he moved deeper into the village in search of Monsieur Philippe and his red door, the houses began to huddle closer again as the road narrowed.

He did not have far to go. A crooked lane ran down one side of the carpenter's house. He heard the obvious sounds of woodworking coming from a workshop lying a few meters to the rear of the house. He aimed his footsteps in the direction of the sounds and the smell of sawdust. At the opening, he peered into the dim interior and saw three men, one bigger directing two smaller. They all wore brown baggy trousers. The man in charge wore a vest and had rolled up the white sleeves of his shirt; the other two wore smocks. All were liberally coated with wood shavings.

The Artist stepped forward and sneezed. The men stopped what they were doing and turned towards the interruption.

"Yes?" the taller man said, impatiently.

The Artist realized that what he had originally taken for gray was dark hair liberally sprinkled with sawdust, which also coated the man's apron and trousers. The two apprentices—for that is what he assumed they were—blinked curiously at him.

"I am the Artist," he said. "I am boarding at the house of Madame Sorel. She said you might help me construct canvases for my paintings. I have a few ready to assemble, so I am in no rush. I would prefer not to send to Paris, if you are able to assist me with future wooden frames. I will need to find a source of canvas cloth as well. Perhaps you can direct me?"

The carpenter thought briefly, and then nodded. "That sounds simple enough, Monsieur Artiste. Bring what you have with you tomorrow afternoon. We can discuss measurements and payments. I have a contact who might assist with the canvas. Nothing fancy though, *hein*?"

The Artist nodded slightly, and the noisy work recommenced before he stepped fully outside.

Sleepiness caught up with him again as he stood at the corner of Monsieur Philippe's and the main road, so he decided to return to his room and rest before braving the café and that evening's dinner. Perhaps some time surveying the prospects from his window might awaken his fingers, and he might be able to begin to draw again. Or even paint. That hope added a spring to his returning footsteps.

4 – The Café

He juddered awake, momentarily confused as to where he was. His stomach growled in earnest. He sat up, rubbing his eyes. His shoes sat beside the bed; his coat lay across the chair in the corner, with his valise and bag of painting supplies next to it. In one sense, this room could be anywhere: a bed, wardrobe, wash basin. But this space was clean and quiet. He could draw a deep breath without pain deep in his lungs. There was a window that provided a view out to the countryside, and not to other rooftops ...

Ah, he was in the hired room in the home of Madame Sorel in the village of A–.

The room stood in semi-darkness. He had slept the entire afternoon away. He stood and walked to the wash basin. Thankfully, his landlady had done him a kindness and filled it with water. He had noticed a pump in the tiny courtyard behind the kitchen. He'd have to go there each day, unless the girl—Gretchen—might be persuaded to do that for him as part of her duties.

A coughing fit struck him—he had gone nearly an entire day without one—so he plunged as much of his head as he could into the basin, blindly grabbing for the cloth to scrub at his severely barbered scalp and face. During his illness, he had grown too shaggy altogether, and so he had instructed Antoine to cut it all away.

Shrugging on his jacket, he patted again at the bristly hair and covered it with his mashed wreck of a hat. He opened the door and stepped through.

A deepening blue colored the sky from heaven to earth, leaving the buildings charcoal smudges. He felt his way down the stairs and trailed his hand along the wall of the house, down the narrow alley, and into the main street of A–. The café was there, a few meters back in the direction he walked that morning. He heard voices and laughter. As he drew nearer, he noticed two tables in the courtyard set out with chairs, but no lit candles. Obviously, the owner did not expect a lot of customers at this time of year. The Artist took a deep breath, squared his shoulders, and entered the café.

An explosion of light, shouts, and tobacco smoke bathed him in a wave of warmth. He flinched as everyone turned to look at him. It was almost enough to push him out again into the anonymity of the evening.

The café was a deep room, with a bar in the back, and a door to the left which presumably led to the rest of the building. Men were seated along the bar and at two small tables which were set by the right wall, next to the lit fireplace.

He cleared his throat. An introduction was in order, and he must be the one to deliver it. Well, if they all wished to stare, he would stare back. "*Bonsoir*, I am the Artist," he addressed the room. "Madame Sorel directed me here to arrange for my evening meals while I am in A–. I am seeking Monsieur Capet."

"I am Monsieur Capet." A giant of a man, even larger than Monsieur Philippe, stepped out from behind the bar. In the smoky air, his features came into focus as he approached. He wore an apron and carried a rag cloth, with his white shirt rolled up to his elbows. The owner gestured to one of the tables. The thin man sitting there and nursing his drink scrambled up and back towards a corner of the room. From there, he proceeded to stand and watch with a frank stare.

A quiet murmur of conversation started up again, but the Artist felt everyone was straining to overhear his conversation with the proprietor. He backed his way onto a seat and stared at Monsieur Capet, who only stared back.

The Arist cleared his throat once more, a throat which now felt ragged and dry. "I would like to arrange dinner each day. What would you charge for such an arrangement?"

Monsieur Capet crossed his arms over the apron. "How long will you be here?"

"A handful of months. It depends upon my painting."

"Upon your painting. I see. Well, dinner is at seven o'clock each evening, except for Sundays, when it's at three. Does that suit?"

"*Oui, certainement.* And the price?"

When Monsieur Capet named a figure less than what the Artist had anticipated, his shoulders began to relax. He had not noticed they had climbed up to his ears, but there they were, and it was a relief to let them go.

"*Oui,*" he said. "That is acceptable, Monsieur Capet."

"*Bien.* One week in advance."

The Artist reached into his pocket, pulled out his coins, and counted out the proper amount.

Monsieur Capet grunted in approval. "Sit here. I will be back shortly with your food. The price includes one glass of wine or beer an evening. Anything else is extra."

Eager to secure the terms and have this giant of a man stop hovering, the Artist tripped over his words in his haste to respond. "A glass of wine, please."

He received a curt nod, and the other man headed to the door at the back of the room. Swinging it open, he advanced down the hallway, shouting out commands which elicited loud responses. The clanging of pots and crockery could be heard until the door swung shut again, and the sounds subsided to low rumbles and dim thunks.

The Artist looked around the room. What felt like a multitude of eyes looked back. But then, assuming the excitement was over for the time being, the townsmen returned to their conversations, though still at a subdued level. The man he had displaced at the table lingered in the corner of the room, sipping his drink and swaying slightly. This was obviously not his first glass of the evening, and he leaned on the wall for support.

The Artist now recognized him as one of the two apprentices from the carpenter's workshop. He nodded a greeting, and the man gazed blearily back. The apprentice looked younger than when he first appeared. His pre-dinner ablutions seemed to have consisted of sticking his head in a bucket of water and sloshing around. His preparations seemingly also included a cursory brushing away of the shavings which still clung to the dragging hem of his trousers and dingy boots. His smock though, was replaced with a well-worn brown jacket. He was one of the few men not smoking.

The Artist continued his visual circuit of the room. The other table was occupied by three farmers, each of whom wore sensible boots and sported a variety of hair colors: blond, red, and dark brown. One of them smiled—if baring one's teeth might be called a smile—keeping his pipe clenched with his teeth as he did so. The others seemed friendly enough and merely saluted him with their drinks. He nodded back and brought his eyes back to the bar itself.

He now recognized the broad shoulders of Monsieur Philippe seated there, along with the second of his young apprentices and a third man with a thick mop of black curls, a tanned face, and blue eyes. Those eyes locked with his and—to his alarm—the Artist watched the man stand, pick up his drink, and make his way to his table. Without ceremony, Black Curls pulled out a chair and sat down.

"I am Jean-Luc," he announced. "But most call me Luc." His eyes crinkled when he smiled. His face was open, but up close the Artist could see the effects of sun and wind giving him a roughened appearance. Another man of the outdoors. His eyes, though, spoke of a life farther afield than the village.

"We do not stand much on ceremony here. You are the Artist. The whole village has been talking about you since your arrival. Has Madame Sorel terrified you sufficiently yet that you wish to leave?" His words were belied by a mischievous grin. He burst into a belly laugh, and the rest of the inhabitants joined in. The Artist couldn't help but join in as well.

Luc reached out and the Artist grasped his hand. "So, you can laugh, Monsieur Artiste," he said.

"Madame is sufficiently terrifying, but I am made of stronger stuff," the Artist replied.

Luc leaned forward and slapped him on the back, which prompted a coughing fit on the Artist's part. At that moment, Monsieur Capet returned, carrying a bowl of steaming meat stew and a substantial hunk of bread. He set them down and then repaired behind the bar to pour wine. Approaching the Artist once more and handing him his glass, he returned to resume his perch, and the evening settled around them.

The Artist scooped up the thick broth, appreciating the generous chunks of meat, carrots, and potatoes.

"I was once like you," Luc said. "Not an artist. A traveler."

Ah, I was right, thought the Artist.

Luc continued. "I went to see the world as well, but now I am home from my wars and farm my land, the land of my father and grandfather. Our roots grow deeply in these parts." Luc leaned forward. "Do you do portraits? Watercolors?" The man raised his eyebrows.

The Artist choked on a spoonful of stew. He wasn't sure if this was sincere interest or mockery. "I work in oils," he said as soon as he was able. "I prefer to work outside. I paint what I see, I paint quickly. My wish is to capture the moment, and to do that, one must work as swiftly as possible. No days or weeks. No salon."

"Ah, you are one of those." Luc leaned back in his chair. "I saw some of them when I was in Paris. Pissarro." He tapped a finger against his nose. "Well, you are welcome to tramp my fields in search of the perfect view, just stay away from my new wheat as it grows, *hein*? But now I must leave. *Bonsoir*, and I will see you again soon."

Luc stood up from the table and gave a whistle. A large, golden dog the Artist had completely overlooked jumped up in front of the fire and followed his master out of the café and into the night.

Monsieur Capet caught the Artist's eye and nodded. The latter suddenly felt as if he had passed some sort of test, and the warmth he initially sensed when he opened the door of the café crept back into the room. Slowly, he consumed the rest of his soup and bread while downing the wine in between mouthfuls. Finally, he rose, nodded at the men still there, and made his departure.

His walk back to his room was more of a relaxed amble. He had a place to construct his canvases in A—. His belly was full. He had received at least an initial acceptance from the local men, and an invitation to visit some of the fields. Perhaps, just perhaps, he would be able to resume his painting.

He looked up at the night sky and let the light from the moon and the bright stars guide him during the short walk home.

Home.

However, as he climbed the stairs to his room, a gust of wind carried his hat from his head into the darkness. He knew he should retrieve it— he had no other—but he would look for it tomorrow. It was a poor thing anyway, and a night out should not hurt it.

5 – The First Morning

The morning spilled through his open window, bright and sunny. The Artist groggily sat up in bed. He followed some motes of dust or pollen as they bounced in the beam of light, connecting the window to the floorboards. The early light revealed his shoes, tossed into a corner. Where were his clothes? Ah, yes, the closet.

He put his feet down onto the chilly floor and walked over to the basin. Filling it from the ewer, he ducked his face and the top of his head in. He slicked the excess water out of the stubble on his head and batted at the moisture clinging to his beard. He then padded over to the door, opened it, and tossed the used water over the edge of the stairs and into the narrow alley—which was when he spotted his hat from the night before. It sat there, reproachfully, in a puddle of his own making. He heard a sudden squawk below, and one of Madame Sorel's chickens clucked its way over, plopping itself down in the middle of the hat's crown, settling contentedly. The hen cast a beady eye around, and promptly tucked itself up for a nap. Now he did not have a hat. Even a man without a care for fashion could see that.

He went back inside. He was eager to begin work. His dreams had been filled with skies teeming with stars, spinning in all directions, and a brightly lit café. If only there were a way to capture sound with his paintings. He felt again his frustration with the two-dimensionality of his art. While using different thicknesses of paint added texture and depth, they could not capture the three-dimensionality of objects, nor the matrix of sound and touch in which those objects were enclosed. But he was trying, and he would keep on trying. He did not know where he wished to begin painting. He needed to feel the countryside more before that would come to him. Yes, he would sketch instead.

He impatiently rummaged through his valise for a clean shirt, yanked open the closet door to scoop up his trousers, and hurriedly dressed. He knew he should tidy his room and set it to rights, but he was overcome by a sense of impatience he could not ignore. He reached into his painting sack for his notepad and pencil stubs, which he jammed into his trouser pockets. He reached back into the bag for another pencil, and his fingers closed on a small, stoppered glass bottle. A parting gift from one of his Parisian acquaintances. His fingers hesitated. It was still sealed; thus far, he had kept his promise to his brother. But he could not risk it being found, so he stuffed it into his coat pocket as far down as it would go and shrugged himself into the coat's sleeves. He flung open the door, locked it quickly, and headed down the stairs at a jog.

Gretchen was standing at the stove when he entered and, wordlessly, motioned him to the table while she went to the sideboard to select a bowl. Back at the stove, she scooped some porridge into the bowl and carried it to him. Next, she poured him a cup of coffee and then went to fetch some jam from the pantry. He gulped down his food quickly.

She stood before him, hands on hips. "Please do not choke, Monsieur Artiste."

In between swallows, he managed to get out, "My lunch?"

She gave him a pointed look but retreated to the pantry. Returning with a baguette and a chunk of hard cheese, she wrapped them in a cloth before handing them to him. Jumping up from the table, he took them from her with a quick word of thanks and darted out the door.

On the main road, he hesitated for a moment to check that he had what he needed, and then looked back at the way he came yesterday, then to his left, at the road out of the village to the south.

The south.

A tune came to his lips, something disreputable, something he had heard outside *L'Opéra* in Paris, and he began to whistle it. He could feel the sun starting to creep up and launch its assault on his head. He would need to buy himself another hat. Another moment of carelessness, another expense.

His brother had provided him with a small amount of funds to replenish his raggedy wardrobe after he had lost so much weight. The Artist could see his brother now, shaking his head, but he had felt too many possibilities today to let the thought of his brother's presumptive consternation weigh him down. He would guard the *francs* his brother had loaned him carefully. And he would sell a painting. Or two or three! Anything seemed possible today. And then the younger brother would no longer have to look after the older one. He picked up his pace to escape the shame that particular thought always caused him.

Soon, he found himself amid fields, rolling before him and to each side. Should he select this field to begin with? Or that one over there? He could not decide; he was spoiled for choice. He just knew that today it would be one of the fields.

He began to feel the bubbling energy but recognized the edge of mania to it so attempted to tamp it down. He must tamp it down. He had work to do. He was almost dizzy with the fact of being so close to putting pencil to paper and then oil to canvas—he could not risk it.

Twenty minutes later, the town completely receded into the background, and he was alone, just himself and the wind. He came to a stop and listened. No horses. No shouts. No crowds of passersby. No steam. No smoke. Just stillness. He closed his eyes, leaned his head back, and as well as he could with hands encumbered by his day's supplies, extended his arms.

He stood that way for some time. It could have been minutes or much longer. He came to when the sun began burning his face and head. Moving slowly and calmly, and cured of his earlier rush, he looked around.

These fields here were currently fallow, and spring planting would be underway soon. To his left, they had been cleared in preparation while to his right, they were still resting, covered in a drowsy green. Beyond the green, a small grove of trees sat at the top of a hill. The Artist left the road and began the slow climb to the summit.

He reached the top slightly out of breath. From that vantage point, he saw the village as well as miles of fields. For a moment, his vision shifted, and he watched the fields cycling through the year. From the newborn fuzzy green of spring through the lushness of summer, into the golden tones of fall, and then the hard brown and black of the soil, sprinkled with snow.

His Eye was awake and ready to paint. Seating himself in the shade, he flipped open his notebook and began to sketch.

6 – Lunch En Plein Air

A throat cleared, and the Artist looked up from his notebook into the amused face of Luc, the man with the blue eyes who had joined him last night at his table.

"*Bonjour*, Monsieur Artiste. You are a very serious man, I can see. I have been standing here at least fifteen minutes."

"Truly?" The Artist blinked into the sun behind the man's broad shoulders.

Luc laughed. "No, not truly. I exaggerate for dramatic effect. But you have been sitting for a while. The shade has moved, and you are beginning to turn—" He squinted. "A rather fetching shade of pink."

The Artist scrambled to his feet, spilling pencils, notebook, and lunch into the grass. Laughing again, Luc reached down to help, and they hit their heads hard enough for the Artist to see actual stars. Reeling, he clutched his forehead and blinked. "I do appear to be rather the fool, Monsieur."

"Nonsense," said Luc, handing him his things. "Allow me to welcome you to my fields."

"These are yours?"

"This little patch, yes. It belonged to my father. When I received news of his death, I returned to take up my patrimony and become a farmer. There are some fates one cannot escape, no matter how far or fast one runs away from them."

The Artist had never owned anything. His father had been a man of business, as was his brother. He himself barely possessed the clothes he wore, and he aspired to only a little more. All that mattered was painting, from merging with his surroundings and pulling them onto the canvas, to the finished painting itself. But *belonging* to a place? Knowing that it was his home and not simply the place he laid his head? That was never a part of the equation for him. But listening to this man, watching him now, he felt a wisp of what it meant to belong somewhere. What might it mean to be able to say, this place is mine, I claim it?

"I am far from home myself," the Artist said. "But I am never going back." He added nothing further.

Luc looked at him with a slight frown but did not probe. As if he were examining me, thought the Artist, as part of his landscape. Or his fields.

He waited for what would come next. As he did most days, the Artist felt himself bristling with a nervous energy, a static electricity that could raise hairs on his arms. In the past, this energy pushed people away. Was it a twitch in his hands? His eyes wandering away in the middle of a conversation? A tendency to silence with sudden outbursts? Or did he speak in riddles, though he made complete sense to himself?

He never knew for sure. So, he waited, anticipating and dreading that moment when Luc would push away. Surprisingly, though, it did not seem to bother the farmer. At least not here, out in the open fields and sunshine. The Artist's breathing slowed, and he was able to fully meet Luc's eyes.

He found the sharp light in the deep blue he had noticed the night before. The man's hair was a lighter brown in the sunlight; in fact, it was a number of browns, with hints of gold and even red in spots. They shifted in the breeze, and he was fascinated by the movement and the changing colors. But he was staring. He dropped his eyes.

"I am eating, just there, down by the brook," was all Luc said. "Please, join me."

Nodding mutely, the Artist followed him down to the tiny stream. As they approached, the golden dog jumped up from where he had been patiently awaiting his master.

Luc knuckled the top of the dog's head. "Bruno," he said and waved the Artist forward. There was a spot where a low tree overhung the water, and he set himself down near a baguette, cheese, and apples laid out on a small cloth. Tearing off his boots and stockings, Luc plunged his feet over the edge into the water. "Come, join me."

Hesitantly, the Artist mimicked Luc's actions, bending down to set out his food and then removing his shoes and stockings. The water swirled around his feet, a coolness running between his toes and causing a pleasant shiver to wend its way up his body.

"I believe I need a hat," he said abruptly. "Where might I find one in town?"

"I have a few hats on my farm," Luc said carelessly. "If you don't mind a lowly farmer's straw hat, I can bring you one at the café tonight."

"I would like that. Yes."

The men sat in companionable silence, each chewing on their respective bread and cheese. The Artist watched the water. Listening to its sound and feeling its coolness, he thought yet again how he might capture all those things, along with the colors of the water and the streambed underneath. He noticed Luc had finished his lunch and had lain back down on the grass. The Artist swallowed the mouthful he had stopped chewing when he began watching the creek.

Luc fished for a blade of grass, placed it into his mouth, and meditatively chewed on it. Bruno wiggled forward and placed his head on his master's stomach. The farmer absently rubbed the dog's head and stroked his ears, seemingly lost in thought. Once the Artist began wiping away crumbs, Luc resumed their conversation.

"I never thought to come back here," he began. "I had my fill of this place. I decided that I needed to explore the big, wide world, so I left my parents and my sister and went to sea. I saw things, many wondrous things. I met beautiful women—" He nudged the Artist with his foot and chuckled. "I had adventures. I thought I was free. But then, one day, I was in Marseille and met a man from the nearby town, the one with the railway station, and from him I learned that both my parents had died, as had my sister's husband. And then I knew my days of freedom were over. It had its teeth in me, this land. I never thought of myself as a man with responsibilities. But responsibilities I surely had then. And so, I returned." He laughed again, though this time the Artist heard a rueful note in it.

Luc pulled himself back into a sitting position. "I have a good life here. I have my fields. I will plant soon, and things will grow. I will never be wealthy—I had to sell too much of this land to cover my brother-in-law's debts so my sister would have a proper chance of survival. *Peuh*, my brother-in-law. He played too often at cards, and not well. But at least my sister has a roof over her head and no mouths to feed. Though whether she finds that a cause for grief or thankfulness, I cannot say. She takes in boarders, to keep body and soul together. You know her. She is your landlady."

"My landlady." The Artist blinked. The thought of Madame Sorel, a stern and solitary figure, having something as human as a brother had never occurred to him.

Luc chortled at the astonishment on his face. "Yes, your landlady is my sister, Madame Sorel. And I am her disreputable little brother." At that, Luc jumped to his feet, scooping up his shoes, stockings, and food cloth—did the man ever do anything at half measures? the Artist wondered—and exclaimed, "But enough ruminating! I must get back to prepare for planting. I will see you tonight, *hein*, at the café?"

The Artist scrambled up as well and bent to retrieve his things. "Yes, tonight at the café. I have an appointment with Monsieur Philippe this afternoon. I wish to begin painting soon."

"Then until this evening, Monsieur Artiste." Luc tossed one of the apples to him and set off with Bruno following at his heels.

Before he was out of earshot, the Artist called, "Why is Monsieur Philippe called Monsieur Philippe? Is that his last name or his first name?"

Luc's laugh carried back to him across the breeze. "That is his story to tell, Monsieur Artiste. Ask him tonight, after he has at least one glass of wine in him. *À bientôt!*"

The Artist watched as the two retreating figures became tiny blobs of black, white, and brown with splashes of gold against the landscape. Some of the morning's warmth had faded, though no clouds impeded the sun. A beam of light hit the dog's fur in just the right way, and it gleamed, but when he rubbed his eyes, the disappearing animal seemed brown.

Tucking that conundrum away for another day, the Artist sat to don his shoes and stockings, retraced his steps up the hill, and headed back down the road towards the village. His fingers briefly caressed the bottle buried deep in his pocket, but he retrieved his hand and stepped jauntily forward, his morning's sketches dancing around in his mind as he decided which to paint first.

7 – An Afternoon and Evening

The Artist returned to his room late in the afternoon after a satisfactory first full day. He spent the afternoon in Monsieur Philippe's workshop, reviewing the ready-to-be-assembled canvases which could be used as models to construct future ones. They had set out a timetable for the next set of canvases and agreed on a price. The Artist was relieved it would not be a large drain on his limited funds.

Monsieur Philippe allowed him to remain in the workshop afterwards to sketch the men working, after instructing him to stay out of the way. The beams of sunlight were filled with motes of sawdust. As the men moved in and out of those beams, he would see how their motion stirred the air, revealing to him a piece of dusty clothing or a flash of browned skin, so that what was air, wood, or man all became part of the same dance. To do this true justice, though, he would need paint. He resolved to return.

Back in his room, he was pleased to see it had been tidied. The floor had been swept, his valise had been unpacked and placed in the wardrobe, and his meager collection of clothing—two well-worn shirts and another pair of trousers—hung on the sturdy wall pegs. His easel had been unfolded and propped up in a corner. He placed his newly assembled canvases in a stack next to the easel; they made a satisfactory inventory.

He suddenly remembered his sack of painting supplies and re-opened the closet to see if it was there. He breathed a sigh of relief. It was. He opened the neck of the sack and rummaged through the assortment of paints, brushes, and painter's palettes. All there. He patted his jacket pocket. Yes, all there. He had been wise to keep the bottle with him.

Dusk had not completely fallen, so he had to wait before his evening meal. He went over to the washstand and lit a candle as the air around him continued to darken. There was a feeling that this room, with its specific furnishings, was uniquely here, and uniquely his. Perhaps this is where he should start before venturing outside with his oils. Here, in this room. In the sunlight, the colors called out and revealed themselves to him. He had experienced his fill of shadows. His fingers itched to pull out a brush and paint. But first, rest and food. Or, rather, food then rest. And then the sun, to make it all come alive.

He rubbed at his bristly head and reached for his hat. That's right, no hat. He had spotted it when he returned, still adorned with the protective bird which squawked again at his appearance and then rose and waddled away, leaving a brand-new egg in its place. Puddle, bird, egg—there was no end to this hat's humiliation. No matter. Either Luc would bring him a hat tonight or he would enquire where he might find one.

The warmth of the café hugged him like a homecoming as he stepped inside its doors. Several men gave him a brief nod and returned to their conversations. Suddenly shy, the Artist simply ducked his head in acknowledgement.

He took his seat at the same table as the night before and looked up to catch Monsieur Capet's ever watchful eye. The publican nodded and disappeared down the hallway, again to the sound of shouts and the clanging of pots and pans.

Sitting back comfortably, the Artist directed his eyes at last to the bar, where Monsieur Philippe, the second apprentice, and Luc were again seated. He took a moment to look around for the thin apprentice and found him leaning in the corner of the room, as if he had been there since the night prior. The young man's eyes were bleary, and he stared at the Artist as if he were not quite in focus.

Luc pushed himself away from the counter and bent down to say something in Monsieur Philippe's ear.

"*Peuh!*" exclaimed the carpenter, but he followed Luc over to the Artist's table.

Pulling out a chair and sitting down, Monsieur Philippe began speaking almost at once. "So, you want to hear the story of my name, do you? Think it is Philippe Philippe or some such foolishness, do you? Hah!" He glared at each of his apprentices, one at a time. "I do not gossip in the workshop. But here, over a drink—" He raised his glass. "Well, I do not mind."

The sound of voices dropped as the carpenter began to speak. The Artist had the fanciful impression that several pairs of ears, not least those of the carpenter's assistants, had swiveled to focus on Monsieur Philippe.

"I had the usual sort of name when I was born—nearly: Marie-Joseph Jonquil. *Hein*! No sniggers there. Look at me. Do I appear a delicate flower? *Non*!" He glared at the room, took a sip of his drink, and continued.

"The *curé* in my home village tried to drum some learning into the thick heads of those of us who lived there. He told us the story of a great Spanish king." He spat at the floor, at which point Monsieur Capet looked up from his polishing behind the bar and frowned in their direction.

"Philippe the Second," Monsieur Philippe continued. "He sent an enormous armada to attack the English, but he lost, goddamn their eyes. Still, it was a larger showing than we French have ever done at sea. Isn't that so, Luc?"

"Well," protested Luc, "we French acquitted ourselves quite well with the American war against the English, for example."

Monsieur Philippe waggled his fingers in dismissal and carried on. "So, I declared I would be Philippe from that day forward, and Monsieur Philippe when I was grown to man's estate. And that is my story." He set down his glass with a firm thump, stood up, waved his hand absently at Monsieur Capet, and headed out with a mumbled "goodnight" to the assembled drinkers.

The Artist watched him leave and when he turned back, Luc was looking at him.

"Well, you have your story," the farmer said.

"*Oui*, I do indeed. *Merci*, Monsieur Luc. It is not what I imagined."

"It rarely is," replied the farmer. His blue eyes gleamed with a hint of mischief, and he gave a half-smile. In the next moment, he suddenly jumped up and walked to the fireplace. He bent down and pulled a sturdy straw hat from a sack, which Bruno was patiently guarding.

"Go ahead, try it on," he said.

The Artist gingerly placed it on his head. It fit well and pulled down low enough to resist the winds. The room erupted in applause. He stood and graced the occupants with a bow.

"You are a proper farmer of A– now," Luc said. "*Bienvenue.*" He whistled for Bruno, tipped his fingers to the cafe owner and the Artist, and then headed out into the night.

8 – Gretchen

Gretchen drowsily listened to the familiar, loud ticking of the grandfather clock two floors below her attic room. That clock ordered her days. She often wondered if it was directing her sleep as it beat out the hours. It was always there, on the edge of her consciousness. Even when she stepped out into the yard to feed the chickens or climb the stairs to clean the Artist's room, she could feel its constancy. It was as if her body had been absorbed into the clock and served as its ticking pendulum. And when the clock struck the hour, she was suddenly awake.

She graced herself with a few more minutes and stretched out. Her hands reached one wall, and her toes touched the other. She turned to look at the small, round window which brought the sunlight into her attic room. The rooster in the yard out back had begun to stir, and his announcement was joined by the other roosters throughout the village of A–, as they sung their grating dawn hymn.

As the summer progressed, her little room would become stiflingly hot, but for now it was still cool, and a light breeze came through her open porthole. She knew it was called a porthole because Master Luc called it that when he came to repair the legs on her washstand once, and he had spent time at sea. "Does my sister run a tight ship?" he had joked. Her confusion must have registered clearly on her face as he explained how the window reminded him of those he had seen on ships.

Over the long years he'd been away from the village, he had seen so many things.

Master Luc.

She had come to know his face so well, she might even be able to trace it in the air before her. The wide forehead. The firm chin. That tiny, upturned corner to his mouth when he was amused, but did not wish his sister to see. Those blue eyes.

The grandfather clock struck the quarter. At the sound, Gretchen leapt from the bed, hurriedly pulled up the sheets and the rough blanket, and plumped the pillow. She checked her braid in the slightly rippled glass that Madame had placed on top of her washstand.

Every night, she carefully unbraided her hair and brushed it for one hundred strokes. It was one of the few things she remembered from her childhood. Her mother—the memories were much dimmer now, and her face was blurred, but the warmth was still there—would hum each evening, while Gretchen sat on her bed. Her mother would count the strokes before carefully re-braiding her daughter's hair and placing a little nightcap on her head.

There was no time today to unplait and re-plait it, so Gretchen carefully wound and pinned a kerchief over it. She tried to wear a kerchief most days—well, most days when the mistress was about. She suddenly remembered the first time she met the Artist and blushed recalling her kerchief had been set aside that day. She had known he might be coming down but decided to risk it. And then he walked in.

A strange man. As different from Master Luc as chalk was to cheese. She noted the lodger was painfully thin, more scarecrow than human. He looked as if he slept in his clothes, and out in the open. His reddish hair stood up like bristles on his scalp. She might have thought him a beggar, until she saw his eyes. His eyes. His eyes saw things. Everything. She gave herself a little shake to push that memory away. It unsettled her.

When he first arrived, earlier in the year, he remarked about the color of her hair and laughed at her name. Yes, he was quite different from the other men in A—. He could be insufferably rude, but at other times, polite and well spoken. A man of education and some means—at least, once upon a time. Now, he was obviously poorer than the mice inhabiting the walls of the house, and she should know, as she tended to his room after he set out each day wherever he had decided to go. She tried to work out a method to what he did or where he went, but the only thing she'd been able to discern was that he dropped things where they fell each night and did not bother to pick them up in the morning.

Except for his paintings and painting supplies. He tended to those most particularly.

He had a little notebook he carried everywhere. She was curious to see what it contained. Perhaps one day he would leave it in his room, and she could take the smallest of peeks. When he left each day, he propped his canvases up, so they leaned towards the wall without touching it. She was afraid to turn them around, to look. Afraid he would notice they had been touched. She sensed a fierceness in him. He was never fierce with her, but there was something there, banked, and she did not wish for that flame to come alive and lash out at her.

Still, she wished to see—both what he sketched, and what he painted.

She wished to see what those eyes of his saw.

Getting ready was the matter of a minute, and then she was tiptoeing down the stairs in her stockinged feet, her wooden pattens in one hand and her house shoes in the other, so as not to wake Madame. The pattens were necessary to protect her shoes from the muddy yard, but their wooden forms made a terrific clacking and clattering sound, so she was careful never to wear them inside. In the kitchen, she sat on a bench and put on her shoes and then the protective pattens before bringing the stove back to life. The dough had risen overnight in the pantry, and she would need to begin the daily process of making buns and baguettes. But first, she took the coffee pot out to the pump in the yard and filled it with water.

She stood for a minute before going back inside, her face turned up to catch the early rays of sun while the chickens pecked and clucked around her feet. She had forgotten the feed. She went back to the kitchen to place the pot on the stove, and then out again to feed the chickens. In the tiny coop, she checked for fresh eggs. The prime layer of the household was still abed, sitting on a beaten-up hat. Gretchen took a moment to stroke the chicken's feathers and run her fingers over the outlines of the cap.

She had found it in the mud, adorned by an egg, and had recognized it as the Artist's. The next day, she attempted to clean it under the pump, to no avail. When she spotted him wearing a straw hat, which he now wore every day, rain or shine, she concluded that even he declared the old hat a lost cause. Apparently, it was to be the hen's property, so Gretchen tucked it into the coop. With a sigh, she stroked the chicken a few more times and then gently reached her fingers underneath and drew out a large, lovely brown egg. The chicken scolded her but settled back into her nest for a longer snooze. "Lazy thing." Gretchen was scolded far less frequently since the hen obtained the Artist's cap to nest on. How funny she was, that chicken, but Gretchen was grateful; it was better than being pecked for her pains.

Soon, it was time for the Artist to descend to the kitchen for his breakfast. He breezed in, distracted and full of energy, clutching a small, pink flower. Its stalk was just starting to bud into the burst of what she recognized as a *sanfoin*.

The Artist sat at the table and stared at the flower, chewing his lip and turning the tiny stalk this way and that, and occasionally holding it up to the light. He paid her no mind as she brought porridge and coffee for his breakfast. He continued to gaze at the bloom while he ate, whistling between his teeth as though, by examining it hard enough, he would discover—what? What would he discover? It was a common, ordinary flower. No rainbows or prisms in sight.

"Monsieur Artiste, your porridge is growing cold."

He startled, stared at the spoon in one hand and the flower in the other. With a bashful smile, he set down the flower and recommenced eating, polishing off his breakfast and gulping down his coffee. Before he left, he cleared his throat and said quietly, "Mademoiselle Gretchen, I thank you for what you do for me. I am—" He waved his hand. "Far better off than I might be, for your care. Thank you for mending my shirt. And fixing that hole in my sock. I do see. And I do thank you. Perhaps one day you would do me the honor of letting me paint you in recompense."

She blushed, and before she could come up with any words, he turned on his heel and strode out. His pockets bulged, meaning there would be no canvases. He was going to sketch.

She began to hum as she cleared away his dishes. She picked up the forgotten flower and gazed at it, trying to see what he saw and felt a fool that she could not. Or perhaps he was the fool. But she couldn't bring herself to throw it into the yard to be trampled by humans, chickens, or other beasts. In the corner of the windowsill, she spotted a pretty blue bottle that seemed the color of a summer sky, when the sunlight was angled just right.

Oh, I shouldn't do this, she thought, but in a flash, she had the bottle and the flower tucked into her apron pocket and quickly—and as quietly as possible—climbed up the stairs to her room. She added water from her ewer to the bottle and then set both bottle and flower on the lip of her little porthole window, so the sun could shine through the glass and brighten the drabness of the room. Maybe she would be able to discover the mystery of the flower.

She had not been quick enough. As she descended the stairs, the break from pattern and the clatter of shoes had brought Madame from the parlor.

"Gretchen, are you well?"

"Yes, Madame. So sorry, Madame. I had forgotten my kerchief in my room." She tugged at it.

Madame Sorel *hmphed*, and the suspicion retreated from her eyes. "See that does not happen again, girl," she said. "You are becoming more forgetful by the day."

Gretchen bit down the retort which still, after all these years, sprung to her lips. Instead, she took a fast breath through her nose and bobbed her head, willing her back and shoulders to relax. Madame could sense rebellion a kilometer off, and Gretchen did not wish to give her an excuse for some type of punishment. Madame's husband might have beaten her; he had, in the old days. After his death, Madame preferred withholding a meal or locking her in her room.

The morning and the midday meal passed. The addition of a boarder meant Gretchen had another excuse—besides market day or running an errand for Madame—for some time on her own. After fetching the key from a hook outside the kitchen, she took a broom, cloth, and bucket, and climbed the stairs to the Artist's room.

Even though he was not there, the Artist's presence lingered. Well, she scolded herself, how could it not? His painted canvases were carefully arranged against one wall, the unpainted piled nearby. His shirt and socks from yesterday lay on the floor in front of the closet. She picked the clothing up, inspecting to see if the day before had left traces as to where he might have been. A few splashes of mud, a smudge of something on the sleeve as if his hand was coated with something when he rolled it up to begin painting. She would set things to rights, would repair any new holes she might find in the socks, and then wash them along with the shirt.

After she swept, mopped, and threw out the water in the basin, she returned for a final look. She picked up the cloth to quickly dust the washstand and the backs of the chairs, again humming to herself as she worked. She fluffed up the pillows and smoothed down the coverlet.

That is when she saw, sitting on one chair, an apple. She moved nearer to examine it closely. It was beautiful. She picked it up and smelled it—delicious. She knew this apple. It only grew in one orchard in these parts, the orchard belonging to Master Luc. So that's where the Artist was. Or had been.

She turned the apple around and noticed that a couple of bites were taken out of it. The pale flesh was turning brown. Slowly, she brought her lips to the bitemarks, shaping her mouth to fit over the same bite pattern, and pressed her lips to the apple. Her teeth sunk into the fruit, through the softening flesh and into the firm whiteness underneath. It was still juicy, and the juice ran down her chin. She froze, shocked by what she had just done. What had she just done? She abruptly set the apple back down on the chair. Would it be noticed, or would it be better to throw it away? He wouldn't notice, would he? He might not or he might call her a thief.

Whirling around, she snatched up the items she brought, along with the Artist's clothes, and fled down the stairs, the empty ewer forgotten. She stopped at the bottom, trying to catch her breath, almost sobbing. She leaned against the wall of the building until she was able to get herself under control, and then returned to the kitchen. With the afternoon tasks completed, she had a blessed hour of freedom to return to her room and rest before she began dinner.

Slowly, much more slowly than was her habit, she climbed the stairs. The door to her room was open. She had closed it, yes? Of course she had closed it. A cold feeling settled in the pit of her stomach. Madame Sorel stood inside with her back to the doorway, looking out the porthole window.

"What is this?" She held in her hand the blue bottle with the flower. So, she had found a way to punish Gretchen for her small break in routine this morning and it was to be this. "I said, what is this?"

"It is ... it is nothing, Madame. Just an old bottle. And a flower. It will only last a day or two. I will return the bottle to the kitchen."

Madame Sorel's mouth set into a thin line. "There is no need for such common, messy things in your room. I run a clean and tidy house. This—" She pulled the flower from the bottle, sprinkling water on the floor. "This is not acceptable." She marched over to the window, opened it wide, and tossed both water and flower onto the yard down below.

"See this doesn't happen again." Madame Sorel strode past Gretchen, the bottle still in her hand, dulled by the shadows in the dim stairway. "In, girl. As I will have my meal with Madame Dufort, I think an evening by yourself is in order." With that, she pushed Gretchen into the room and pulled the door shut.

Gretchen heard the key turn in the lock.

Hardly daring to breathe, she collapsed onto the bed. She buried her face in the pillow; sobs wracked her body as she cried without sound, a skill she had mastered through necessity. This day she felt lost, unmoored, in a way she had not felt in many years. Soon, she was pulled into sleep, while the light through her window dimmed, then blazed briefly with the colors of the sunset. And all the while her body kept track of the chiming of the grandfather clock.

When the Artist climbed the stairs to his room for the last time that evening, filled with one of Monsieur Capet's satisfying meals washed down with a hearty glass of beer—after a day spent sketching the people of the countryside hard at work, it was only fitting to drink something more nourishing than wine. Wearily, he noticed the ewer had not been filled with water. Perhaps Gretchen was ill. But then his mind returned to which sketches called out the loudest, and which ones he wished to transmute to oil and canvas. As he mentally flipped through them, all thought of fresh water and housemaid disappeared.

He would find the discarded flower the next morning, muddied and torn, when he went to fill it up at the pump. However, the story of how it came to be there was not his, and remained part of the town of A–, in which he was still but a newcomer, no matter his straw farmer's hat and his days turning into months amongst the villagers.

9 – Funds – Monsieur Capet

Though he had passed a sleepless night, the Artist waited until a suitable hour to make his way to the café. He carried a letter in his pocket addressed to his brother, begging for more funds. He hoped he wouldn't have to post it today.

It seemed odd, opening the familiar café door to meet a largely silent room. Windows that he had somehow never noticed were open, their shutters fastened to keep them from swinging. The only person inside was a young woman with dark hair and a determined expression, vigorously sweeping the floor. The chairs and stools were stacked on top of every available surface. She looked up as he entered, her broom in mid-sweep. He set down what he was carrying and immediately snatched the straw hat from his head.

He hesitated on a form of address—was she a young wife? A grown daughter? A maid of all work? His lips came together in the shape of the "M," when she resumed her sweeping and called out in a piercing voice, "Capet!"

"*Allors*," came the response from the hallway, down which the café owner retreated each evening in search of a plate of food. The Artist now recognized the woman's voice—it was the sound that accompanied the clashing pots and clanging cutlery from the kitchen.

Tutting impatiently, she indicated sharply with her head that he was to proceed. As he stepped forward, she noticed what he was carrying. She called out again, "L'Artiste!"

As if that was his cue, Monsieur Capet emerged from the door to the hallway and into the café. His eyes widened at the sight of the Artist. He opened the door to the hallway again, and this time, the Artist stepped through.

The dimness of the house's interior momentarily blinded him after the brightness of the open-windowed café. The Artist tripped slightly in response, but he swiftly regained his footing and continued after Monsieur Capet, past the kitchen, and then making a sharp right into what was a plain but comfortable parlor. Well-worn furniture—a couple of armchairs and a settee all brushed to within a centimeter of their lives—filled the small room. Two small vases with flowers sat on a windowsill and a side table, respectively. The walls were bare of ornament, save for some vivid wallpaper and a paper silhouette of a redoubtable woman wearing a cap.

He was relieved when directed to a chair with its back to the forbidding silhouette. But even then, his words died in his throat, and he could only sit there, gazing down at his hands and the canvases gripped within them.

"So, Monsieur Artiste, to what do I owe the pleasure?"

The words were spoken abruptly, but kindly. The Artist clung to them, using them as a ladder to pull his proposition out of his mouth.

"Monsieur," began the Artist, "it has been my great pleasure to partake of the evening meals you provide in the café for these past months. I would like to present, again, my compliments to you and to the cook."

Monsieur Capet nodded, his eyes narrowing.

The Artist cleared his throat. "I am, alas, at a period in between funds as I await the sale of some of my paintings in Paris. There is a buyer, I am assured, who will shortly finalize his purchase." He began to sweat slightly. He never was good at lying, but the buyer was a possibility, had always been a possibility, even if said buyer had never materialized. "Therefore, I wondered if I might secure your interest in purchasing these paintings or, rather, use them as payment for my future meals?"

Monsieur Capet sighed. The matter had been broached; the words spoken. The café owner sat back in his seat, then leaned forward, resting his elbows on his knees and tapping his pursed lips. The Artist's heart sank as he waited for the dismissal.

However, after a few more minutes, Capet indicated the Artist should set out his four canvases, so they might be viewed. Gratefully, he stood up and placed them around the room, against the walls where he could, and on the settee.

Monsieur Capet stood and moved out of the way to allow the Artist to do this and, as if he were a patron at a gallery, he began his circumambulation of the room. He stopped before two of the Artist's pieces, breathing heavily for a moment, and then resumed walking. He ended directly in front of the Artist again.

Indicating the Artist was to retrieve his canvases, he made himself comfortable until the Artist was seated once again, with the paintings propped against his legs. "Monsieur Artiste," he said, "you have been a good customer these past several months. You have paid on time, you have not been drunk or disorderly, and you get along well with the other patrons. These are marks in your favor."

He tapped at his mouth again, and then resumed, "But you know A– is not a wealthy place. I do not have rich patrons. Frequently, it is a struggle to keep my own family fed and the wolf from the door."

The Artist's heart continued its plummet, which had reversed with hope during the viewing.

"I cannot give you money for these," Monsieur Capet said. "I know you work, and work hard, and these—" he wagged his fingers at the canvases, "are the result of that work." He pursed his lips and tapped at them again. "What I can do is to take, say, three of them as a surety for the next six weeks—a fortnight for a painting. Then, when you have secured funds, I can ascertain where I am with my own budget, and we can negotiate which you reclaim and which I retain as payment for your meals. Does that suffice?"

Six weeks! Six weeks was a lifetime. It was a window, with some hope at the end of it for an actual sale here or even in Paris. He swallowed. He needed that window. "*Oui*, Monsieur Capet. I agree to your terms. Which are the three canvases you wish to retain?"

"The painting of my café. The one of Monsieur Philippe and his men, that is Monsieur Philippe, is it not? And the sunflowers. My wife may like that one in our parlor. They are very odd looking, Monsieur, but they do brighten up the room."

The Artist selected those indicated from his stack, shook the café owner's hand, picked up his remaining canvas, and made his exit. Madame—or perhaps Mademoiselle—Capet was completing her sweeping, and she used her broom to sweep him out and onto the front step.

One down, one to go. And if he thought Monsieur Capet was a mountain to climb, what was his next stop, an entire range?

He returned once more to his room to select the four canvases he wished to bring for the next visit, and then reluctantly made his way to the front door of his landlady's house. He hesitated on the front step, his hand set to knock. Should he go to the kitchen, like a tradesman hawking his wares, or should he present himself at the front door as a gentleman? He stood, frozen, hand raised, as his brain jumped from one option to the other. It was in that less than prepossessing pose Gretchen found him, as she opened the door to do a final polish of the front door knocker—a brass fixture of which Madame was inordinately proud.

Her hand went to her mouth in a surprised giggle and the Artist found himself blushing to the tips of his ears. But she swiftly recovered herself. "Are you well, Monsieur Artiste? Would you like a cup of coffee? We have fresh rolls in the kitchen, if you would like to go back with me. It is irregular, but perhaps Madame would not mind."

"No, no, thank you. It is Madame with whom I wish to speak."

"Oh." She glanced down at the canvases clutched in his hands. "Oh." She hesitated, clearly unsure of what to do. "Wait here. I will see if Madame is at home."

The Artist stepped inside, and Gretchen closed the door behind him. She went and knocked on the door to the front room, entered, and shut the door. He heard muffled voices; one sharper than the other. Gretchen returned to stand before him.

"Madame says you are to enter. Five minutes only, Monsieur."

The Artist nodded and moved forward. He heard a faint "good luck," but as his head moved to catch the sound, Gretchen was already hurrying down the hall to return the polishing cloth to the kitchen, door knocker forgotten.

10 – Funds – Madame Sorel

Madame was seated formally in a high-backed chair, next to the spindliest of tables, on which rested a steaming cup of coffee and one of the pastries she was proud of making by hand. She had left her apron off. In its place, she had set a napkin on her lap to catch any crumbs. The look she bestowed was far from warm. Her eyes deliberately strayed to the coffee and pastry, then back to him. She sighed and rested her hands on the napkin. A finger began to beat time to the loud ticking of the grandfather clock out in the hall.

He found himself absorbed by the overstuffed room. It was as if the space was breathing, pulsing in time to his heartbeat. Or was it the clock? The light in the room was dim, with the drapes drawn shut and the wallpaper richly colored and dark, though faded in places. The Artist thought he also detected, low down in one corner, a black smudge as if ink or blacking had been hurled at the wall.

And he was staring again. The silence in the room took on an ominous tinge, as it usually did around Madame. Her lips tightened in the familiar way, but this time, a tiny quirk lifted one corner, as if she were enjoying the effect she was having on his nerves. Somehow, this gave him the courage to speak.

"Madame," he began, "I have been your lodger for a few months now, always circumspect in my behavior and timely in my payments."

She gave the slightest of nods but said nothing.

"I thought ... I thought, Madame, that you might wish to see what I have been working on since I came to be under your roof, so you have proof of my industriousness. And, if you should desire any of my canvases as a memento of my time here, I am sure we could come to an arrangement."

At that, she stirred. "So, you are leaving me, then?"

"Oh, no, Madame. I misspoke. I wish to continue my time here. The countryside has done wonders for my health and has excited my muse in ways I have previously not experienced. I have been ... that is, the paintings ... I am, in short, inspired."

"I see." Silence once again descended.

"So, Madame." He shifted on his feet. "Here are some canvases I thought might appeal to you. One is of your house. One is of the road from the train station through the village. Lastly, this one, this one here, is a portrait of my room." At this, he lifted his head, which had been focused on the canvases as he sat each in front of her.

"Your room?" she asked. "Of what possible interest might your room be, to me or to any person?"

"It is an example of life, Madame, an impression of the ordinary. Our daily lives have value. They do, Madame." He pulled out that particular canvas and set it out before her.

"But what have you done to the room, Monsieur? I am renting you a clean, serviceable space, maintained simply and to the highest standards. What are these colors? These dabs? These swirls? Monsieur, this is not art."

"I beg to differ, Madame. The ordinary, the everyday, contains so much life and where there is life, there is energy and art. The simplest object is filled with a myriad of colors and movement. Nothing is still. No, everything vibrates. That is what life is, Madame. That is what it means to be alive."

"*Peuh*! This is not art, Monsieur. I am not sure what it is, but of that, I am certain. I pride myself on being an arbiter of taste. Though I live in a tiny town in what some may call a backwater, I have taste, and I do not like being made a fool. I could not put any of these up on my walls. No, I am not interested in the canvases you brought with you. *Absolument pas*! I would ask that you leave my parlor and not disturb me again with this so-called *art*. I have never seen the like, Monsieur. Please leave and take your paintings with you."

The final *coup de grâce*: "And please do not forget your rent is due at the end of the week."

With that, she returned her attention to her cup and the pastry. Clearly, the interview was over.

An old, familiar weight settled on the Artist's shoulders, stooping him forward and pulling his chin down. A tremor started up in his hands and a great force of will was required to calm them. Quietly picking up the canvases, he gave a courtly bow to Madame Sorel and shuffled his way out.

He stood on the front step, unsure of where to go next. The day was not far gone. In fact, there was still enough time for him to take his notebook and his luncheon and sketch. Yet he felt as if he had just lived through twenty-four hours. Or forty-eight. What was he to do now? His head was full of *francs* and *sous* and having to write to his brother to say he had, once again, failed. No, today there was no space in his head for sketching.

He heard shouts and turned his head to watch a gaggle of boys tear down the main road of A–, obviously let go early from school demands for the day. Swinging their books, slates, and lunch pails, they whooped to one another. Where were they going? Never mind. Most of the boys had passed when the Artist spotted the two boys he had seen that first day. He knew who they were now—the son of Monsieur the Mayor and his friend.

The Mayor.

The Mayor!

A dim hope began to flare, and a thrumming ran through his veins.

The Mayor. Perhaps not all was lost yet.

He raced up the stairs to his room and frantically searched through his completed canvases, identifying four he thought might prove just the thing. Then, snatching up those, he raced down the stairs and almost sprinted to the other end of the village. The Mayor. Perhaps.

As he had flipped through the canvases, however, a faint buzzing had begun to grow in the dim reaches of his mind. It hummed of Paris and its voices. Of failure, jeers, and mockery. And the approach of bees. But they were still far off, so it was easy to dismiss the sound.

11 – Funds – The Mayor

The Artist carefully made his way to the Mayor's house, the most imposing residence in the town of A–. It stood by itself, not leaning into or over any other dwellings, with a small garden around it and a white graveled pathway leading from the gate to the front door. A variety of native orchids lined the way, adding a splash of color to the walk.

Carefully, he set down two canvases to lift the gate's latch, straighten his collar, and brush away any remaining smudges and stray souvenirs of the prior day. He realized he should have made himself more presentable back in his room. He felt his hat was too common a thing to bring to this interview, so, he left it behind.

There was nothing he could do about the condition of his face. His skin never truly darkened. As a redhead, he was too fair to properly tan. Therefore, his face frequently blistered and even peeled when he spent too long in the sun. He often forgot his hat, hurrying as he did to capture a scene completely before it disappeared into something else—or something separate from his vision of it. But recently he had remembered the straw hat, and his skin had a healthier hue.

Taking a deep breath, he pushed open the gate and walked up to the imposing front door. Without giving himself another moment to hesitate, he set down two of the canvases again, picked up the heavy knocker, and let it pound once, and then twice.

He felt quite alone at that moment, on the stoop. But the freshness of the air, the circuitous path of a bee flying from one end of the garden to the other, passing close enough to hear its hum, the conversations of the birds, and chattering of small animals just outside the garden's walls, all combined to remind him he was a part of this life, right here and now. He clutched the passel of canvases a little more tightly to counter the almost unbearable itch to grab for a brush and paint.

As he lifted his hand to grasp the knocker for a third time, the door opened to reveal a tidy housemaid, with dark hair carefully tucked under a cap and a crisp apron covering her striped dress of blue and gray—not the usual black. She had the smallest puffed sleeves, and she seemed to pose herself in such a way as to set them off to the best advantage. "Monsieur?" she asked, as she took him in from head to foot.

"Mademoiselle, I am the Artist. I have business with Monsieur le Maire."

Her eyes, the brown of bark, widened slightly. "Please, Monsieur, come in," she stated. She held the door open and stepped aside.

The Artist looked around the high-ceilinged space. It was not too different from his parents' home. The floor was of highly polished wood, with an intricate carpet stretching from one side to the other. An arrangement of orchids sat on a large table, next to a bowl for receiving calling cards or more elaborate *cartes de visite*. A grandfather clock ticked away the minutes to his right, near a door to another room and a stand filled with umbrellas and walking sticks.

He supposed, if the doors to all the rooms were open and the drapes pulled back, it would be a sun-filled space. He wished it were now. It seemed too hushed and muffled, and he found his heart synchronizing with the clock's beats, though in his own chest they felt heavier and heavier.

"Please wait here, Monsieur," the housemaid instructed. She gestured with her arm, rather forcefully, to emphasize that he was to remain where he was, and then she disappeared down the hallway.

A quick scuff from above caused him to look up. There, at the top of the staircase, was the tall, young lad he had seen on his first day in the village. Perhaps it was a sign? He didn't believe in signs. Well, he would take an omen, any omen, to speed him forward. "*Bonjour*," he said.

"*Bonjour*, Monsieur Artiste," replied the boy. He left his perch at the top of the stairs and slowly made his way down, stopping about halfway. "You see," he continued, "I did not forget. Are those your paintings?"

"*Oui*, they are. Some. But you have the advantage—you know who I am. Who might you be?"

"I am Claude-Joseph, the son of Monsieur le Maire. The *only* son of Monsieur le Maire." And then, as if his visitor might not completely understand, he added, "I am an only child."

"I see," stated the Artist. "Well, Claude-Joseph, would you like to see my canvases?"

"Most certainly." The boy came down the remainder of the steps and stood directly before him. The lad was neatly dressed, though he had left his jacket and cap presumably up in his room. His dark hair was carefully combed except for an unruly cowlick, which stuck up in the back. "What is this first one?"

"It is the grove of trees just beyond the village."

"Ah, I see. But I would not have recognized them, Monsieur. They twist far more than the real ones, which are rather plain. And these appear to be almost dancing. Trees do not dance, Monsieur, they stand still."

"Well, Claude-Joseph, they may appear so. But if you observe them closely, with all your senses, throughout the course of a day or days, you will see that they do move. They are very much alive."

"A canvas cannot breathe or live, Monsieur Artiste. A canvas is an inanimate object. I have studied the differences between living things and non-living things and those that are in-between, such as plants or flowers. They are distinct."

"Then we will need to agree to differ. One day, I hope to show you, out in the world, what I see."

The boy fixed a skeptical eye on him, as though his tightly woven animal, vegetable, and mineral classifications of the world and the people around him had begun to un-knit but were encountering resistance.

"There are more things in heaven and earth, Horatio, than are dreamt of in your philosophy," the Artist said softly.

Claude-Joseph opened his mouth to respond, but any chance of further speech abruptly ended. At that moment, a door at the back of the hallway slammed and the maid re-emerged. "Monsieur! The Mayor will see you in his study. Please follow me." She caught the boy's eye after she spoke and indicated with a jerk of her head that he needed to return to the upper floors. "Quickly," she breathed, "you are not supposed to be downstairs, young master. Run along before you are discovered."

As Claude-Joseph turned to plod his way upstairs, the Artist gave him a helpful smile. Then he followed the maid to her master's study.

12 – A Meeting with the Mayor, continued

He was ushered into a small library, where a fire burned in the fireplace despite the warm day outside, and heavy velvet drapes shut out the light. A perspiring and rotund figure sat at an elaborately scrolled wooden desk. His balding head gleamed in the heat, and an enormous set of mutton chop whiskers extended his cheeks by two or three times. He was clearly engaged in some type of important task, as he grunted a bit and whistled between his teeth as his pen scratched the paper before him. An elaborate, multi-colored waistcoat strained around his substantial belly, in contrast to the soberness of his jacket and the whiteness of his collar and cuffs. He ignored both the maid and his visitor until he finished what he was writing. Then, he set down his pen, turned around in his chair, folded his arms, and fixed his gaze on the Artist.

His gaze was penetrating, a thorough review which took his visitor in from the crown of his head to the toes of his scuffed work boots, much as the maid had. The Artist initially met the Mayor's scrutiny but then dropped his eyes, not wishing to present a challenge. The humility of begging for a commission tightened his grip on the canvases, putting them in danger of being speared with a finger. But then he remembered the letter in his pocket ready for mailing and addressed to his brother. He let out a breath and pulled his shoulders back, standing as straight as he could. He slightly lifted his eyes again and saw that he was still subject to that shrewd gaze.

"Well," said his interviewer, and reached with his right hand for a fat cigar which was burning in a dish on his desk. Waving the retrieved cigar between thumb and finger, he directed the Artist to sit on what could only be described as the petitioner's chair, a trifle more threadbare and lower in the seat than the other chairs in the study and the only one lacking arms, but not so poor in quality as to reflect badly on its owner. "You are the Artist."

"*Oui*, Monsieur le Maire."

The Mayor took a couple of deliberative puffs on his cigar, sending out rings of smoke that drifted down and over the Artist's face. He coughed slightly.

"You want something of me, Monsieur Artiste."

It was a statement, not a question. How he responded would direct the Mayor to treat him as a common laborer or a man of sensibility, and possibly worthy of grudging respect.

"I wish to introduce myself, Monsieur. I have met many of the inhabitants of A– during my months here and have the good fortune to be a tenant of Madame Sorel."

"Most excellent, *oui*, most excellent. *Hmmm*. Yes, well, I have been travelling. Business interests, you see. Opportunities for our good *ville*. A mayor today cannot afford to sit and wait for the world to come to him. No, he must go out into the world. These modern times are changing at such a pace, *hein*? If we are to thrive, and perhaps attract additional business and industry here, why, that will be all the better for everyone involved."

"*Oui*, Monsieur, I do understand. My father and brother travel frequently for their business, and I myself have lived for many years in Paris. The world is transforming and doing so quickly. The marvels continue to appear at a pace so rapid that even in Paris, people are often astounded."

"And where are you from originally, Monsieur Artiste? I detect traces in your speech which are not of our region, or of Paris. I pride myself on my ear; it has stood me in good stead these many years."

"I am originally from the Lowlands," replied the Artist. "I learned quickly, however, if I wished to advance in both technique and artistry, I needed to be where the best artists in the world were. That place was, and remains, Paris."

The Mayor nodded. "While I would not dismiss the many advantages of A–, it cannot compete with Paris as a center for the arts. That is true. So, then, what brings you here, so far away from your *milieu*?"

"I have a weak chest, Monsieur, and the last winter in Paris caused me much distress. Illness interfered with my ability to paint. I thought the fresh country air, along with new vistas and images for inspiration, would best heal me both physically and artistically."

"Well, it *is* a healthful place," replied the Mayor. "I had not considered it before as a therapeutic respite." He turned around in his chair, pulled out a fresh piece of paper, dipped his pen into the inkwell, and began to scribble a few notes.

The Artist looked around. It was a relatively tidy room, though without the rigid precision of his father's. Books and ledgers filled floor-to-ceiling bookshelves on two walls, and the cheerful fire crackled along the third. The desk sat along the fourth. A settee and two more comfortable chairs were grouped in front of the fire, a space where more casual chats could take place. However, this was a business discussion, at least for now.

The Mayor laid down his pen and swung around. His right hand still clasped the cigar, which was burning down substantially and would need to be snuffed out soon. With his free left hand, he fluffed out his whiskers.

"Ideas, Monsieur Artiste, always ideas. Time waits for no man, yes? We must always be awake, ready to seize the moment."

"*Oui*, Monsieur le Maire."

"But now that the pleasantries are over, let us get down to business, *hein*? What is it you wish of me? Surely not a letter of introduction?"

"No, Monsieur. I wish to show you some of my paintings, in case you would be interested in purchasing them for any of the rooms in your fine house. Or you might wish to view them as samples and commission a painting."

"Ah, we get to the meat of the matter, Monsieur." The Mayor took a couple of final puffs on his dying cigar. "Yes. Well, my late wife—God rest her soul—was the true appreciator of the finer things in our household. I am a plain man, a businessman. I view things in practical terms. Therefore, I do not see myself acquiring new artwork for the walls of my home. Every picture is a memory, Monsieur, don't you know."

"*Oui,* Monsieur, I do." He paused and swallowed, looking for another approach, and remembered the boy. "But you have spoken of yourself as a man aware of the future. And I have met your son—a fine young man. I hope I do not presume when I state that you wish him to be well equipped for the world we are rushing into. My painting—" his hands shook slightly, "—is part of the future, Monsieur."

"*Hmmm.* Well, set them out for me."

The Artist arranged his paintings around the room. This time, he had chosen portraits to display: two of them from life, one from sketches, and one from memory. The Mayor stood, smoothed his waistcoat, and began a circuit of his study. The cigar was jammed back into his mouth, almost extinguished now but a convenient thinking tool gripped between his teeth.

After one turn, he returned to his seat and gestured for the Artist to resume his. He plucked the cigar out and set it down on the small plate. "Well, Monsieur, as I said, I do not possess an eye for art. That was the province of Madame, my wife."

The Artist felt his stomach plummet again. His hands, now free, retreated to his pockets, where they caressed the bottle, which had made its home there.

"I do not need any of these artworks for my walls. No, I do not. But you have given me an idea. It is right and fitting that a leader of the community should have a portrait, do you not think? Something for the people in the *ville* to note. Yes, note. I also lack a portrait of my son. I would like a commemoration of him, of his youth. He will leave me all too soon to continue his studies and take up his place in the world. I would like to have a reminder of this most precious time, yes? Also, it is right and fitting that a young man of his status should have a portrait made of himself. Yes, that is good. Yes."

The shrewd eyes, which had been gazing out to an imaginary future, re-focused on the Artist.

"Are you able to do two portraits, then? One of me and one of my son? The cost will need to be reasonable. This is not Paris. We are not, ... well rather, ... we are solid, upstanding, moderate people here."

The relief the Artist felt was tremendous. He was buoyant, unsure whether his feet were still touching the ground. He paused, afraid his voice might be as high and floaty as he was feeling and that would never do.

"*Non*, Monsieur. Proper, sensible, and true. Yes, I will paint you and your son true to life. And the price will be quite modest." He named a figure, less than he would have asked in Paris, but still more than he dared hope.

The Mayor thought for a moment, then nodded and stuck out his hand. "Then shall we shake, like the English, Monsieur Artiste." Again, it was a declaration and not a question. "When can you begin?"

"As soon as you would like, Monsieur."

"Two weeks from today. You can start with my son's portrait and then do my own." He tugged open one of the desk drawers and counted out some *francs*. "Will this do as a deposit?"

"*Oui*, Monsieur."

"I will write out a receipt for my records." Pulling out a fresh sheet of paper, he picked up his pen again, and signed a brief agreement, along with the deposit paid. He gestured for the Artist to sign. Blotting it thoroughly, he pulled out a folder from a corner of his desktop, tucked it inside, and then inserted the folder into one of the desk's pigeonholes.

"*Bien*. Our business is concluded. I—that is, my son—will see you in two weeks, Monsieur. The maid will see you out."

With that dismissal, he returned to the stack of papers and folders on his desk. The Artist stuffed the money into his trouser pocket, gathered up his canvases, and retreated from the room as swiftly and silently as he could. Out in the hall, the maid had disappeared. He waited a moment for her to reappear, but when she didn't, he let himself out. He was saved. For now. He was saved.

When he returned to his room, he carefully added his completed paintings to the other stacked ones and pulled the letter to his brother from his pocket. He wanted to tear it into little pieces and toss it into the muck of the yard, but that seemed a temptation to fate he was not willing to make. Instead, he smoothed it flat and tucked it into the back corner of the wardrobe and set his case over top, where it would remain, a constant warning.

13 – Apples with Luc

"Monsieur Artiste, I thought you told me ten minutes? One haystack does not a farmer's living make! I must get back to my tasks. And all the squinting you are doing—you look quite fierce. What happened to the hat I gave you?"

"I was in a rush this morning to capture the light."

"I cannot say the persistent squinting becomes you, my friend, but you have joined us farmers in the woody quality of your skin. Well, more red than woody."

The Artist gestured impatiently with his brush to keep Jean-Luc in position and the farmer subsided once again, though with a sigh. "Hurry up, then," he said. Bruno was present as usual and entertained himself by darting about the haystacks, returning frequently to check on his master, and then darting out again.

The Artist worked quickly, too impatient to sketch first. He mixed his colors swiftly, thickly, and boldly, as if he were desperate to catch the scene in front of him before it was lost. Luc watched his attempt to relax the squint, but the absence of his hat and the direct sunlight soon had him squeezing his eyes fiercely again at the painting, dabbing and jabbing, looking from subject to palette to canvas.

From months of observation, Luc had learned the Artist was now unreachable, and conversation would be fruitless. He willed himself to relax. He was worrying about the wheat crop in the far field and the corn and barley in the closer fields, though the hay was coming up nicely. He knew he could sell and barter some of his crop locally and use a portion for his animals and himself. It was the larger market which concerned him. You could never depend upon it. This is why he had taken to chewing on pieces of hay from the stacks he was beginning to assemble; it kept him from grinding down his teeth. He missed the days when all he needed to make his way was to rely on his strength, nimbleness, and—if absolutely necessary—quick thinking. He exhaled.

Dependency on others did not become him. It caused an itch between his shoulder blades that sometimes made him want to claw his way out of his own skin. If it got to be too much, he spent an evening at Madame Bertrand's. When it became unbearable, he would disappear into Marseille for a couple of days and drink himself into a stupor. Regardless of how far he strayed, however, he knew he would come back. He always came back.

He had felt no true ties when he set off to see the world all those years ago; he thought he was free of all—land and people. But then a tug came and when it did, it was powerful, enough to take his breath away. He could not have resisted it if he had tried, and he did try. He tried for two weeks, but that pain, as if a dog had sunk its teeth into the back of his leg, did not let up. It had throbbed, day and night, and only lessened when he planted his feet in the direction of home. Home? Yes, home. He supposed that was what A— was now.

He snuck a look at the man working feverishly before him. The Artist had taken up his invitation to roam his fields, and the man had spent many days painting views of the various corners and open spaces of Luc's family's land. Some days, he'd nod or wave in greeting across the field. Other days, they would share their lunches, largely silent, except when Luc found himself narrating another part of his life he was not used to talking about. Or when the Artist would abruptly state whatever was randomly going through his head, which usually was completely unconnected to anything Luc had been saying. The master of the *non sequitur*. But Luc had grown used to it and the uncertain rhythm of their communication. It had become comfortable, and he was doing much better at suppressing the occasional shout of surprise at the Artist's interjections. Much better, yes, but they still slipped out on occasion.

Some nights, Luc joined the Artist at his table in the café. Other nights, he simply raised his glass in greeting and continued his conversation or argument with Monsieur Philippe or one of the other *habitués*. Yes, it was a friendship, but an odd sort of one—very different from the friendships Luc had known in the past. The man did not put on airs, though he was obviously a *bourgeois* and had been well educated.

Luc himself had a hungry mind, barely fed by the village school. He'd been able to fill it as an adult by seeing the world and reading. His house contained a small, but carefully cultivated, library. Why, he was known to sit down with Monsieur le Maire to discuss issues affecting the wider world, and the Mayor had spoken to him like a fellow *bourgeois*. He, Luc, former sailor and farmer!

The question of happiness was one he had set aside when he returned to A–. He faced the cards he'd been dealt and lived his life. He hadn't realized he was lonely until the Artist arrived. It was the absence of loneliness in his presence that led Luc to measure the depth of his own unhappiness. Luc wondered if the Artist was ever lonely. He seemed self-contained most of the time, so it was hard to tell.

This train of thought suddenly caused the itch to rise between his shoulder blades. Seeing the Artist, being around him, had kept it at bay for several months. This self-reflection, sitting under haystacks, not getting in his crops, not getting anything done—he jumped up.

"*Mon Dieu!*" exclaimed the Artist. "I am not quite finished!"

"Monsieur Artiste," rejoined Luc, politely but forcefully, "I am not one of your Parisian models. I have things I must do." Then, with even greater emphasis, he added, "I have already given you far more time than I can afford." He whirled on his heel to leave and heard the grumbling start from the Artist.

"It would have been only a few minutes more. Such a rush, always. Perhaps I have captured all I need to move forward. It is meant to seize a moment, to be a thing of one particular and specific instant. By drawing it out too long, I am losing that moment. So, yes, yes, you may go. Yes!" The Artist's words had been slowly ascending in volume, until the last burst out as a shout.

The two men froze. As if he were a marionette, Luc stiffly turned around to face his friend. They looked at each other. Something had shifted. Some energy had solidified between them, without them fully comprehending what it was, aside from having an awareness it was there.

Luc broke the silence. "Monsieur Artiste, I am sorry if I spoke too hastily. I must return to my work. The crops ... they are ready for harvest for such a brief time." He paused. "I can offer you a slight recompense, however. I have been too attached to my plow, scythe, and pitchfork of late, and you have been too attached to your canvases. We need a night out, a chance to chase our various worries away. Come with me to a quiet house outside the railway town, which is the establishment of Madame Bertrand. We can have a hearty dinner there, and then enjoy other ... entertainments. Yes, yes, I insist. And I am happy to have you as my guest."

The Artist waited, and something crossed his face that Luc could not name but which almost seemed like a type of terror. The Artist batted at his ear, as if an insect buzzed too closely. He wet his lips, coughed a couple of times, and then said, "All right. I will come."

"That's the spirit! Yes, we will go, we will shake the dust of A– from our feet and return reinvigorated. You shall be able to tackle even more canvases, perhaps even at a faster pace, *hein*? I may not see you tonight at the café or over these next few evenings, I must tend to work so I can escape for one night, but I will meet you outside the café four days from now, at six o'clock."

With that, Luc strode away from the painting and the afternoon. Bruno abruptly ceased his games and ran to his master's heels. Before disappearing into the landscape, the farmer turned briefly. "Monsieur Artiste! Catch! Hah!"

Reflexively, the Artist lifted his hand and caught one of Luc's omnipresent apples. Then he returned his attention to the canvas.

14 – Madame Sorel Senses a Threat

Madame Sorel adjusted her shawl around her shoulders. She missed the days when her husband provided her with a sweet little trap and a well-behaved pony to take her to neighboring towns and villages to visit friends. But those days were long gone. She sometimes asked for a ride from Monsieur Adam—the farmer two fields over—but he was busy with his crops. She knew her brother was as well and did not even bother to ask him. So here she was, walking back home on the hot and dusty road after a comfortable afternoon drinking tea and gossiping with Madame Balibar.

Her feet hurt. Her head hurt. Drops of sweat rolled down her back. The pastries she had brought, her pride and joy, had wilted a bit in the heat of the walk over, and so were not at their best when she unveiled them from their carefully wrapped home in the basket. Madame Balibar had been full of stories of crop failures, milk cows drying up in the heat, and the loss of her neighbor's baby. The hours had gone quickly.

But the visit was over, and it was time for the trudge home with nothing enjoyable at the other end. Madame Sorel had provided Gretchen with strict instructions on the preparations for that evening's dinner, but she feared they would not be followed, or something would go wrong with the preparation, and she would be disappointed in that as well.

At least her lodger was not any trouble. She must keep an eye on Gretchen, however. There was no point in her getting ideas of anything untoward; young women filled their heads with romantic twaddle these days. Why, in her basket she had one of the latest novels from Paris, courtesy of Madame Balibar.

She abruptly stopped to take a breath at the perimeter of her family's fields, and a flicker of unexpected movement caught her eye. Next to a prominent haystack, she spotted two figures. One was the Artist, painting again. At least you could verify his industriousness. She was glad the entrance to his room was outside so she would not be disturbed by any odd hours he might choose to keep. Mostly, he had woken up early and retired early—nothing to complain about. But he was not painting, he was standing, brush poised and gesticulating at the canvas. And there, when he should be tending to his crops, lounged her brother.

Well, not lounging perhaps. He was standing, but his semi-relaxed posture contained a contradictory quality of intensity, as though energy was being held in check and could spring out at any moment. Whatever the two men were discussing, it seemed very important. But what could they possibly have to talk about? There was a connection between them. Was it anger? They were so tied. She frowned, perplexed and uncertain. And then, for the briefest of moments, they held themselves immobile, like insects in amber, and the world around her seemed to take a breath. Even the sound of the wind across the grass and through the leaves hushed. The rustling of little animals was silenced. Then the world started up again, and her brother departed with a wave and tossed something—perhaps one of his apples—while the Artist returned to his canvas.

Something had happened, but she did not understand. Suddenly, she was the one who was angry. Why was her brother wasting his time, putting his crops in jeopardy, to while away his moments with this Artist fellow? He needed the money; she needed the money. If the two men were to fall out and her lodger were to leave, she would lose this small income. Or, if the fellow were truly angry, perhaps he would not recommend the village and her boarding situation to his other artist friends back in Paris, and then where would she be?

These men and their lack of practicality. These men and their moods.

She knew her brother became restless. She knew he would sometimes take off for a few days, even a week, but he always returned.

Yes, since the first time, which she now referred to as The Return. This Artist ... he made her uneasy. What ideas was he filling her brother's head with? Would the man's talk of Paris and cities cause Jean-Luc to shake off the village of A– and return to the wide world, disappearing from her life, once and for all?

She needed to prevent that from happening at all costs. A bead of sweat traced a pathway from under her bonnet and down her cheek. She would need to find a way to keep him here. She remembered—was it two years ago?—when she came across Luc and Gretchen in the pantry. It was apparent what was on the cusp of happening, but she put an end to it. She would not have those types of things going on in her home. She was a respectable woman and any servant in her house would maintain that respectability. And as much as she loved her brother, she would not have him toy with the girl and then cast her off. Where would she— Madame Sorel—be, if such a thing were to happen? Gretchen was far from the perfect servant, but she had trained the girl since she was tiny, and everyone knew it was getting harder and harder to find good help. All the young women were going to the big city these days.

But, maybe, as a means to tie Luc to this place, Gretchen would do. It was beyond time for her brother to settle down and start his family. She dared not call it love, love was for the romantics in the silly novels she borrowed from her friend. But a combination of lust and practicality might work. It would mean losing Gretchen to Luc's home. No, they could always find a way for Gretchen to look after both houses. Yes, that might work.

She resumed her walk home, rearranging the pieces of the plan in her head, first setting them out one way and then another, but striving, always striving, to keep her brother here, on the farm, bringing in the money. Especially, most especially, not leaving her alone. That last thought hit her across the forehead as though someone had swung at her with a thick tree branch. She stumbled, but quickly righted herself and proceeded to stifle it, bury it, digging deeper and deeper to find a place where it could not rise again.

This Artist, what was he making her do, how was he making her think? He was disrupting her life, that's what it was. He was disrupting everything.

But she still needed his money and if he were to leave, he needed to depart happily and with recommendations about the House of Madame Sorel to the artists and denizens of Paris.

She had a lot of planning to do. Planning and watching.

15 – The Artist and the Boys

On the doorstep of the Mayor's home, the Artist gave himself a quick once-over. He had requested Gretchen's help with brushing out his coat, repairing a couple tears in its fabric, and helping him rub out the paint stains on the collar and cuffs of his shirt. He wore the straw hat, sad thing that it was—though not as sad as the first one he had worn in the village. He wet his index finger and smoothed down his mustache and beard. There, ... presentable. He brought the knocker down firmly on the door.

This time, he did not have to wait or knock again, as the tidy housemaid opened it so quickly, she must have been quite close. "Please come in, Monsieur Artiste." She led him up the central staircase and into a sunny room with a large window, plenty of warm morning light, and Claude-Joseph just over the threshold.

"Monsieur Artiste," the boy stated formally, standing at attention in what must have been his best suit, highly starched and so stiff he could barely move. "You are to paint my portrait today."

"Yes," replied the Artist. He stepped forward, looking around to see where to set up his easel. The room clearly served as a schoolroom or study—perhaps formerly the nursery, updated to reflect the changing status of its inhabitant. The walls were painted a rich blue, with a glossy white molding. The windows were open, and light flooded the space. Two comfortable, overstuffed chairs sat in front of an unlit grate, with a sturdy, well-polished desk beside the window.

"Monsieur?" Claude's voice cracked slightly, revealing the child still present in the freshly scrubbed young man trying to be as mature and dignified as possible. "Does it suit?"

"*Oui, oui*, Monsieur Claude-Joseph. It suits indeed. First, I would like to do a sketch of you seated at the desk. Then I would like to paint a quick impression of you, perhaps in front of the window to capture the light. We will probably need at least two more sessions to complete the formal portrait, but yes, this suits well."

The boy broke into a glad smile. He was clearly excited to have his portrait painted. "*Bien*," he said. "I am ready to begin."

The housemaid gave a little sniff—the Artist had forgotten she was still in the room—and addressed Claude-Joseph. "Since your father is away, you do not have to take luncheon in the dining room. I can bring something, if you wish?"

"*Oui*, Marie-Josette. Please bring something for Monsieur Artiste as well. We may need to paint right through the luncheon hour. There is much to be done when preparing a portrait."

The Artist stifled a slight smile, ensuring that it was gone completely from his lips when the housemaid turned sharply to look at him.

"I shall do that, Monsieur Claude-Joseph," she said. "But you must not overheat or overexert yourself. And you—" She looked at the Artist. "Please do not do anything to upset or overextend the young master." She turned to go.

"Wait, Marie-Josette. Monsieur, I tried to anticipate what you might need. There is a pitcher of water there, if you need it for your painting supplies. I also set that small table, just there, for you to use. Is there anything else you require before we begin?"

"No, Monsieur Claude-Joseph. You have been most considerate. I work in oils when I paint, but it is most thoughtful of you to have anticipated as much as you have."

The boy gave a nod of satisfaction and turned to Marie-Josette, who curtsied and left the room.

"Oh, Marie-Josette!" he called after her. "If my friend François should call, please send him up here directly." He turned to the Artist. "I told him about having my portrait painted and he was most interested."

"Is he the companion I see you with most days?"

"*Mais, oui*. We are bosom compatriots. We have many plans for the future. He may have a different path set out for him. My father wishes me to become a man of business and his requires him to study medicine. His father is the physician for A–, you see."

"Ah," answered the Artist. "I do see. Now, let us have you sit, just so, yes, there. One elbow on the desk, your head forward, looking out—yes, that is it exactly. Let me begin my first study."

The Artist found Claude to be a companionable subject. He was not a talkative boy, but when prompted, he was quick to respond and seemed an eager but uncertain spirit, trying to find its feet. The boy attempted to maintain a dignity befitting to his position in the world of A–, but he still possessed a youthful curiosity that broke through as the morning progressed.

The Artist completed several sketched studies before Marie-Josette returned with a covered tray for the luncheon. She placed it on the small oval table that squatted between the two armchairs in front of the unlit grate. The boy briefly stole a look at the Artist, who nodded, making Claude jump up and cross to the food. As if he had been released from a straitjacket, thought the Artist, but his small smile retreated as that word brought back a memory he did not wish to revisit.

Over their food, Claude chatted freely and asked the Artist questions about his life—where he was from, how had he made his way to Paris, and what was Paris like, truly, as he had only been one time with his Papa and his *Maman* when he was small. All he remembered of the city was the noise, the people, the trains, the carts, how smoky the air was in some streets, and how the boulevards widened to engulf everyone.

The Artist found himself relaxing and enjoying himself. His own inner boy responded to the non-intrusive but energetic questions. All too soon, however, the meat, bread, and cheese were eaten, and glasses of lemonade drunk, and it was time to get back to work.

"Now, Master Claude Joseph, I wish to do a quick painting of you in oils. This is not the formal portrait, but an opportunity to capture you impressionistically. That is, who you are here and now, in this room, on this day, with the light and the air just so, and your feelings coming through."

"How will you do that, Monsieur?"

"You will see. Now, please stand here. Yes, one hand on the window ledge. Look out at the tree. What is it that you see? Really see it. Smell it. Imagine what it tastes like. What are you hearing? No, don't say anything, only think it. And now I will start painting."

While the boy had escaped for a moment to visit the water closet after their lunch, the Artist set up his easel and a blank canvas. He knew what colors he wished to begin with on his palette and he squeezed them out. The boy obediently took the position the Artist requested and was soon trying hard to do all the older man asked.

After some time, a footstep sounded on the wood floor and the boy whirled around. "François! See! I am being painted. It is simply a moment captured—not the official portrait—but the Artist will use it. Oh, Monsieur, I have broken my pose."

The Artist waved with the brush and resumed painting—yes, it was that moment, the excitement of seeing his best friend, which carried the sunshine into the room along with the emotions of the boy. "Just there, stay there," he instructed. Claude-Joseph obediently froze, but the delight did not disappear. The colors, the movements, everything began to flow through the Artist's eyes and his brush, onto his canvas.

He lost all sense of time. When he came to himself, the sunshine was lower and dimmer than when he started. His subject was wobbling a bit with the effort of holding his pose for so long. The Artist immediately felt apologetic. "Oh, pardon me! I lost track of the time. I hope I have not overly fatigued you."

"No, no, Monsieur." Claude-Joseph looked at his friend, who remained largely where he initially stood. "This has been most exciting. Who would have thought? But, yes, I am a bit fatigued." He went to sit in a chair in front of the fireplace. His friend followed him and took the other one.

The Artist cast a quick eye on what he had done. Yes, it would do, it would do. He began to pack up his supplies—paints, charcoal, pencils, sketchbook—and folded up the easel. The boys watched him, silently and intently. Finally, he had gathered everything and turned to leave.

At that, both boys stood. Claude-Joseph was slightly crumpled after the long day, but doing his best to maintain his dignity as the subject of an official portrait. François, slighter and dressed more casually, watched with large eyes, chewing on his lower lip. He had remained silent throughout; clearly, he was the observer and follower of the pair.

"May I return tomorrow to begin working on your actual portrait, Monsieur Claude-Joseph?"

"*Oui*, Monsieur Artiste. The same time shall be good. My father is away the rest of this week. He says you are to paint me this week and him next."

"*Bien*. Then I wish you gentlemen *au revoir*. Have a pleasant evening. Until tomorrow, then."

"Oh, Monsieur!"

"Yes?"

"May I see?"

Reluctantly, the Artist set down his things, picked up the painting only, and held it carefully away from his body so the drying paint did not smudge.

The boys looked at it, intently.

"This, this is me?"

"*Oui*, Master Claude-Joseph. It is you. At a particular moment in time."

"This is me." He reached out a finger as if to stroke the face and then snatched his hand back. "*Merci*, Monsieur Artiste. Until tomorrow."

The Artist left, grateful for what had been a much more enjoyable experience than he had feared. He preferred being outside when he painted, or doing interiors that involved his own surroundings, or the self-portraits that gauged his mood and allowed him to try out new ideas as he strove to capture the life he saw and felt. He had worried that he would have been required to hold himself in check today, to hold his Eye in check, and produce something more traditional. And he would still need to, at least with the formal portrait. Yet, there was a way in. He had been foolish to doubt how his Eye would be able to help him. Capturing that moment at the window, when the boy had spotted his friend—

drinking down that moment and spilling it onto the canvas made his heart sing.

And the bees had stayed away from his ear all day and were blissfully quiet.

Until tomorrow.

16 – At Madame Bertrand's

Then it was the evening to visit Madame Bertrand's with Luc. The Artist washed his face and hands thoroughly, brushed both his head and beard, and then took the brush to his coat for good measure. Looking at his sun-blotched face in the speckled glass and at his uneven, self-trimmed beard, he grimaced. He would never look the gentleman. He was clearly still the despair of his father. *Bah!* It would have to do. Besides, he was out in the country; who would be weighing his gentlemanly, cosmopolitan qualities here? But he decided to leave his straw hat, even if that meant he would have to go bareheaded, a solecism which gave him a momentary pause. "*Peuh!*" he exclaimed. "Enough, Artiste!"

He stepped onto the landing and carefully closed and locked the door. He checked his pockets, and the little notebook was there, along with two pencil stubs. To be outside without them would make him feel naked, worse even than being without a hat. He reached down further. The bottle was there as well, still unopened. He had kept his promise, but his fingers caressed it, tempted to drag it out and unseal it. His heart thumped in his chest. "*Peuh!*" he said again and turned to head down the stairs.

He was greeted by a familiar laugh. "If that is to be your mood tonight, Monsieur Artiste, perhaps I need to re-think our outing."

The late afternoon shadows revealed his friend Jean-Luc, standing at the end of the narrow alleyway, headed in the direction of the café where they were to meet. Luc had taken some care with his dress—a fresh, collared shirt, a dark blue jacket and dark blue trousers—and a thorough brushing and oiling of his curls gave him a much more sophisticated look than the farmer the Artist was used to seeing. The Artist realized his ears were flaming for being caught talking to himself. He moved down the stairs at a fast clip and gave a little jump over the spot where a puddle had formed after a brief rainstorm. The sky was clear now and the cool breeze was moist with the perfect amount of nip to accompany a long walk.

"My mood is fine, Monsieur Farmer. I am only disappointed that I am unable to look quite the man about town as you are."

"*Touché*, Monsieur Artiste, *touché*! But where is your hat? I do not know whether I can be seen in the company of a man without a hat."

The Artist responded with a look, which caused Luc to burst into laughter again. "Ah, so you do not wish to appear the country bumpkin in your straw *chapeau. Bien, je comprends.* But as the bestower of such an august element to your wardrobe, please note that I am offended. Well, let us shake hands in the English way and begin."

The Artist gave his friend a little bow, held out his hand, and the two men shook. Luc retrieved the small lantern he had set on the ground, and they began their walk to the establishment of Madame Bertrand.

They headed north out of the village, passing the café and a few villagers who were taking care of their final tasks before supper time.

As they passed the Mayor's house, the Artist said, "So, I have painted the son of Monsieur le Maire. Yes, it has gone well. He—the Mayor, not his son, *bien sûr*—has commissioned me and I am to paint the Mayor himself in the coming week."

"Congratulations, my friend! A commission is good, a commission is well. Then your art will grace the walls of at least one home in A–. You will not be forgotten, *hein*?"

"Well, yes, I suppose. It is good to get a commission while I wait for further buyers in Paris. My brother continues to speak to possible leading individuals. He has several of my paintings to share, but it is slow work."

"Yes," replied Luc.

They continued on their way in companionable silence. The Artist listened to the sounds around them: footsteps slapping on the hard-packed earth, wind soughing around their heads, the evening birds crying, faraway shouting from A–.

The Artist's heart rate slowed. He breathed in the evening's scents of lingering rain, dirt of the road, and that indefinable scent so prevalent in this corner of France. They called it *la garrigue*—a mixture of shrubs, herbs, and flowers that created an aroma that swirled around the Artist's feet in a near visible eddy and filled his nostrils until he felt nearly drunk with it. The buzzing in his head quieted; the bees that lurked there went to sleep. It was peaceful, being in this place, with this man, and peace was not something the Artist was familiar with. He drank it in as though it were an element in *la garrigue*—feeling it, tasting it, wondering where it came from and how long it would stay.

Though they were not walking quickly, they soon approached the railway town. The main street was paved, and it felt odd to sense something other than packed dirt under his feet. The Artist had not ventured frequently to this place. As they walked through, Jean-Luc greeted an occasional person with a touch of his cap and a quiet *"Bonsoir."* A few cast curious glances at the Artist. It was getting on to supper time and people had places to go. The Artist was not enough of a figure of interest to catch their gazes for long.

And then they were through the railway town and out the other side. The road here was flanked by ancient, twisting olive trees. In a few places, the gnarled and leafy branches met overhead, blotting out the failing light of the sky and covering the two in splotches of inky blackness.

But Jean-Luc did not light the lantern. "Almost there now," he said. "It is a little way out of town."

A hiccup of a lane opened on their left and the farmer veered. In a matter of moments, he was pushing open the small gate leading up to what had once been a large old farmhouse. A lit lamp hanging by the front door revealed a hint of the building's yellow paint and a corner of green shutter. They headed up the pathway, took a moment to brush off the dust from their footwear—Jean-Luc handed the Artist a handkerchief to brush off his shoes—until the farmer rang the bell. They could hear it bonging solemnly inside and then the door was opened by a young woman with strawberry blond hair, a welcoming décolletage, and a shy smile.

"Mademoiselle Louise! How lovely you look this evening." Luc swept his hat from his head and, in a graceful movement, continued the sweep into a bow. "I am here with my friend, the Artiste."

Louise gave a slight dip of her head and smiled. "Please come in," she said. "You have good timing. There is still a table available, and Cook has made a ravishing ragout."

"Then we have come on the right evening indeed. Please, Monsieur Artiste, follow Mademoiselle Louise."

The two men stepped inside, and Luc closed the door behind them. Gas lighting gave the wood-paneled hallway a warm glow. The Artist looked around. He saw that the furnishings were simple and in good taste—no sight of grime or dirt anywhere. The faint smell of polish came to him, and the distant smells of the supper. Louise led them past three or four closed doors, and then opened one on her left, revealing a small parlor with a modestly sized circular table in front of a fireplace.

The table was set for supper with crisp white linens, sparkling wine glasses, and an arrangement of lilies displayed in the center. "Please, Messieurs, be seated. I will let Madame Bertrand know you are here, as well as the kitchen. The food should be here soon and the wine even sooner. Please." She swept her arm in welcome. Once she saw they were seated, she stepped out, turning to give a smile before she shut the door, leaving the two men alone.

"See, Monsieur Artiste. We may be a humble community, but Madame Bertrand's is one of the finer establishments I have encountered anywhere on my travels. She insists on cleanliness, both for the house and for her mademoiselles. She is most particular."

"I can see that, Monsieur Jean-Luc. It is finer than many of the establishments in Paris. You were kind to invite me. It makes for a change of scenery." He looked around the room: velvet wallpaper, shaded lamps, a black marble fireplace, and the Aubusson on the floor.

A discreet scratching came at the door, and then the proprietress entered. "*Bonsoir*, Monsieur Jean-Luc! It has been an age! We thought you had forgotten us! I am so pleased to see you." Both men stood. She presented her cheeks to be kissed and took both of Luc's hands in hers. She peered at him with attentiveness and a caring which, if it was feigned, made her the equal of one of the actresses the Artist had seen on the Parisian stage. Her thick, chestnut hair was lightly streaked with gray and swept into the latest hairstyle, and her gown was simple yet elegant, a rich hunter's green which complemented the remaining touches of gold in her hair. Madame was obviously someone who kept abreast of Paris fashion.

She dropped Luc's hands to look at the Artist. "But who is your friend?"

"Madame Bertrand, may I present the Artiste, who has come to A— for a time in order to gain inspiration for his drawings and paintings and to escape the miasma of Paris."

"Ah, but of course. We are simple folk here, Monsieur Artiste, but this is a beautiful country in these parts. I hope you are finding the inspiration you have been seeking?" The last was posed as a question. The Artist found himself warming to her, in spite of his nerves and the slight buzzing which had started up again. He felt himself appraised by a pair of bright, hazel eyes. Her face was lightly lined and expertly made up. The faintest aroma of violets surrounded her when she moved. Perhaps the evening would not be as bad as he feared.

He gave her a simple bow. "I have, Madame, I have. I find A— and its countryside to be most inspiring, restful, and healthful. I have never done so much painting as I have over the past few months. Tonight is truly a gift. You have a beautiful house."

Madame Bertrand gave a light laugh and patted the Artist's hand. "Now, Monsieur, you are most welcome. And you must kiss me on each cheek, yes, just so, and now we are friends. Sit, sit, gentlemen. The kitchen will have your food in a few minutes. We have the most delectable wine for pairing. Then I shall return to discuss your evening's entertainment."

With that, she turned and swept out of the room, the jet beads in her ears and along the bodice of her dress making a slight clacking noise—why had he not heard it when she first entered, the Artist wondered. Ah, the buzzing had receded again. He and Luc were alone for a few moments, when the young women reappeared bearing a bottle of wine, with bowls of the ragout and freshly baked bread. The women whisked in and out while the men ate, appearing at opportune times to remove finished plates, until nothing was left but the final cheese plate and the paired wine for that course.

"I do not know if I can eat another bite," observed the Artist, leaning back in his chair and staring with wonder at the rounded mound which was his normally concave stomach.

"Ah, but you must have some of Madame Bertrand's cheese. She is famous in these parts for her cheese, along with, well, other things. But her cheese truly is fabulous."

So, the two men ate, drank, and then clipped the cigars provided and began smoking. The Artist coughed but dutifully took a few puffs and found, surprisingly, that it settled his stomach for once. During the course of the evening, as the night deepened outside, the fire had been lit and gave off a warm glow and the occasional friendly snap. Both men comfortably sagged in their chairs, eyes drooping slightly, once again companionably silent.

The Artist was the first to clear his throat. "Thank you for the gift of this evening, Luc. It has truly been what the doctor ordered. I am relaxed and replete and happy, yes, happy. *Merci. Milles mercis.*"

"You are most welcome, my friend," returned Luc. "But the night is still young." He resumed puffing on his cigar, squinted slightly, and then began blowing out smoke rings.

17 – Later that Night

For the Artist, the meal ended far too soon. Mademoiselle Louise and another young woman with light brown hair becomingly pinned up into an elaborate knot entered the small room. This time, however, Mademoiselle Louise was wearing a lacey peignoir over a nightgown, and her companion was dressed the same. In the light from the hallway, their forms were carved out as silhouettes through the thin fabric. Luc gave a contented sigh, slowly rose, and threw the stub end of his well-chewed cigar into the fireplace. "Mademoiselle Louise, Mademoiselle Marianne, you are both enchanting this evening."

The women gave a slight curtsey and stood, inside the doorway, waiting. Luc eyed each of them, then turned back to his friend, who was still seated. The warmth of the evening was receding inside the Artist, as though the tide was going out and pulling his insides with it, leaving him cold. His head felt fuzzy and his belly full, but the food was turning into a frozen lump at the bottom of his stomach. The faint buzzing had resumed.

"Mademoiselle Marianne, the pleasure is all mine," Luc stated, turning back to face the women. Marianne tucked a stray wisp of hair behind her ear and reached out her hand. Luc took the end of her fingers to his lips. With her leading the way, they left the room.

The Artist had not moved.

Mademoiselle Louise stepped in closer to the table. "Monsieur Artiste?" A slight frown creased her forehead, and a touch of concern clouded her eyes. "Monsieur?"

He looked up at her. The gas jets had been dimmed in the room and her face was accentuated by flickers from the fireplace. They made her reddish curls alternately brighten and fade, an irregular pulsing. He watched her heart beating at her throat. His gaze focused on it, and he matched his own breathing. This calmed him and helped bring him to his feet. "Mademoiselle," he hoarsely said and dipped his head.

She smiled then, lips curling upwards over remarkably tiny teeth. "Please come with me, Monsieur."

He took her fingers in his, raised them to his lips as Luc did, and allowed her to lead him out of the room, down the hallway, to the stairs. The wallpaper seemed to bubble and flicker in waves, the gas jets providing a constant and gentle hissing, and the floor felt as if it were rolling under his feet. When they reached the stairs, he grabbed hold of the banister to keep his balance as they climbed. Concern once again crossed Louise's face at his brief stumble.

The climb up the stairs seemed to take an age. His body did not feel quite his; his legs and arms moved mechanically, as if he were a marionette. "Make it be all right, please make it be all right," was his only clear thought. He silently chanted it, as if the chant would bring order to his breathing and the world back to normal. Heavy food, wine, and cigar smoke enclosed him in a box made of rippled glass, with everything outside him wavy and distorted. The head of the stairs perversely receded in front of him as he climbed; a dark tunnel lurked at the top. As they moved forward, he could hear a dim voice in his ear that grew louder with each step. And then she was there before him, and it was that night again—that night with the artist's model and current resident of Madame Dulac's, Aurielle, with the fiery red hair. A favorite of his at that establishment. Until that night when she and the room and, "*Urghhh.*"

The harsh guttural sound stopped Louise in her tracks. "Monsieur?" It sounded almost as if an animal made a noise next to her and she peered into the dim hallway, for they had reached the top of the stairs.

The Artist shook his head. This was not Aurielle. This was not Paris. This was another time, another place, and another young woman. Perhaps, yes perhaps, she would be able to break the spell.

"Pardon, Mademoiselle. I am not quite myself. The food, the wine, the cigar—I am not quite myself. I did not mean to startle you."

She smiled quietly at him again. "*Je comprends.* All will be well, Monsieur. We have the whole night. We are almost there. This is my room. Please, Monsieur, enter." She pushed at the door and pointed with her other hand.

He stepped into a space that was simple, but furnished in quiet taste, like everything in this establishment, in this remote town. An ample double bed, a fire that was already lit and warming the room, a chest of drawers in one far corner, and a small table and chair with a bottle and two glasses in another. A medium-sized carpet covered the floorboards in front of the fireplace. All looked clean. The candlesticks gleamed from polishing. The fireplace was well blacked. He tried to release the breath he was holding. His ribs were tight.

Louise stepped in behind him and shut the door. As he stood there, she took his arm. "Madame prefers we turn down the gas and use the candles. But it is your decision, Monsieur. This is your evening."

"Candles, *s'il vous plait*," he said in a whisper.

"Of course." She began to move about the room, turning down the gas and lighting the candles. Only then did she say, "Please, sit," and motioned him to the bed.

He stumbled onto it, embarrassed by his clumsiness. The cold in the pit of his stomach crept into his limbs. Pins and needles. The buzzing increased, just slightly, and he could dimly hear Aurielle's giggles, though they seemed to be changing now, becoming agitated. Oh, God, don't scream. Please God, don't scream. He waved against his ear, slapping it lightly, desperately wanting it, her, whatever tormented him, to go away.

"Oh, Monsieur. But you are shy. No worries. I shall be gentle." Louise stepped in between his legs and kissed him, adding a slight bite to the end of her kiss. Her breath was warm, her lips slightly chapped. "Or maybe not? But we shall have fun, yes?" She reached up her hands and unpinned her hair, which fell to her shoulders.

His breath escaped him in a rush. "Aurielle," he said, and reached up a hand to touch one tight whorl of her hair.

"And who is she, Monsieur? Well, I can be your Aurielle, if you would like. Or I can be someone else. Did she do this? Or this?" And she followed each query with a little nip, her hands giving a gentle tug at his shirt until he broke away and tore it off. "Ah, Monsieur," she said, bringing his hands to her breasts. He felt their softness through the fabric. "Here, Monsieur." She untied the ribbon holding the peignoir closed, to reveal a nightgown of almost translucent muslin. The Artist let out a faint groan.

He stared at her breasts, the nipples pressing against the gauzy fabric as it rose and fell with her breathing. The buzzing in his ears grew louder. She picked up his hand again and brought it inside her gown. "There, Monsieur. Does that not feel better?"

He could feel the blood running up and down through her body. He could feel her heartbeat pulsing under his fingers. He felt his own breathing catch and link with hers, so that they were breathing in tandem. It felt as if the entire room was breathing with them, that the entire room was contained in this pulsing, as if he were nothing but their two heartbeats. Or was it one?

Louise bent her head to kiss him again. He felt his lips melting into hers and opened his mouth, allowing her tongue in. He breathed her in. She smelled like lavender and perspiration. "Ah, Monsieur, I think you are ready." Gently, he felt himself pushed down to the bed. He was straining against his trousers and her hands covered his. She moved to help him undo the fastening.

"*Oui*, Monsieur, *oui*." Louise was crouched above him and then she wasn't. They were together and he was in her. Or was she in him? He could no longer tell the difference. He felt himself begin to ... disintegrate. He was their movement, he was one with the energy being generated between them, there was no longer a him, a he, a separate entity. The buzzing grew louder, and he was lost in it. He was part of the rush, the wind, the motion he tried to capture in his two-dimensional canvases. He was joining it, he was a part of it, there was no separation between him and anything else. He was being swept away. With the fragments of consciousness that remained, he became aware of words he could not distinguish and then a scream, which rose higher and higher and wouldn't stop. Why won't it stop, was his last coherent thought. Please, please make that screaming stop.

18 – Even Later that Night

At some point later in the evening, Luc's energetic explorations of Mademoiselle Marianne were interrupted by a piercing scream and the sound of sobs and frantic cries from a nearby room. "No! No! It is too—I cannot stop it! I cannot!" The words became a babble, rising to a shriek. It made the hairs stand up on his head. Marianne pulled away, huddling in the corner of the bed, dragging the sheets with her.

Just then, the door slammed open, and Mademoiselle Louise was panting inside the room, face drained to a chalky white, eyes wide and terrified, her peignoir wrapped tightly around her shivering body. "Monsieur, your friend. He ... he ... he ... " Her teeth chattered and she was shaking all over. Any teasing insouciance she normally carried was gone. He empathized, though; that screaming was unearthly, as though the mouth of hell suddenly opened in their midst. He was not a superstitious man, but he found his hands making the sign of the cross. Doors all along the upper floor began to open and wide-eyed women and their clients peered out.

At the end of the hall, Madame Bertrand emerged with a decorous cap covering her hair and a respectable *robe de chambre* enclosing her from head to toe. She stood outside the room the Artist was in, almost directly across the hall from Luc. The other women clustered around, a sea of lacey wrappers and loosened hair. Madame went to each in turn, placed a hand on their shoulder, and said a quiet word. Reluctantly, the women returned to their respective rooms, their clients following, and one by one, each door closed.

Madame stood in the now empty hallway. "Monsieur Jean-Luc, please put on your trousers. We must see to your friend."

The sobs were softer now, but still audible. While Luc pulled on his discarded breeches, Madame did a quick once over of Mademoiselle Louise. "He did not hurt you, *ma petite*?"

"*Mais, non*, Madame. All was well, all was usual, and then he began thrashing about and screaming, and I could not get him to stop!" Louise dissolved into tears, making Luc aware that under her polish and carefully cultivated coquetry, she was still very young.

"*Bien.* You are well, then. Monsieur Jean-Luc, please take all your things with you. Louise, you are to stay the night in Marianne's room. Come, come, we do not have time to waste. I run a house with an impeccable reputation. We cannot have the gentlemen disturbed by scenes such as this. Come, come."

In a few minutes, Luc found himself in the hallway, clutching his shirt, jacket, shoes, and his lantern, which he had decided to take upstairs with him and not leave in the vestibule. Madame Bertrand looked at it askance, but he lifted it to prove it was unlit and she nodded. Taking a deep breath, the first sign of any discomfiture she had shown, she turned the knob of Mademoiselle Louise's door and stepped inside, gesturing to Luc to close the door behind him once he had entered.

Two candles burned on the chest of drawers in the small space, and the Artist was curled into a naked ball across the room, huddled on the floor next to the bed. His sobs were quieter now, but they continued as he rocked back and forth, periodically punching himself in the head. Unaware of their presence, he repeated, "Stop! Stop! Stop! Stop! I cannot think! Stop!" The bed sheets were ripped clean away and the pillows thrown about.

Madame Bertrand looked at Luc. "I depend on you, Monsieur," she said, "to control your friend. Take as long as you need. But you must be gone before first light."

Luc nodded. Without another word, she turned and left, shutting the door softly—but firmly—behind her.

Luc slowly approached the bed, until instinct urged him to back away, and he stopped, frozen with indecision. Then he remembered a young cabin boy on one of his ships who was prone to nightmares and sleepwalking. The crew learned how to calm his agitation and help him back to his hammock without fully waking him. Perhaps the Artist's current condition was similar. Holding onto that memory, Luc took a deep breath and stepped forward. He reached out a hand. "Monsieur Artiste."

The Artist howled and pulled back.

Luc recoiled at the strength of the reaction but recovered and crept closer. Facing the Artist, who was tightly huddled and avoiding his gaze, he tried again. "*Monsieur—mon ami. Mon ami.* It is Luc. I am here." He eased himself down to the floor. "*Mon ami.* I am here." Once again, he dared to reach out a hand. It lightly touched the Artist's knee. He waited for the man to spring back, but this time he did not. Instead, he quieted slightly. Feeling bolder, Luc moved closer, this time touching the Artist's arm. "*Mon ami*, I am here. I am here."

"The buzzing—it will not stop. It will not. It is all moving, and I am swept, I am being pulled apart, I—."

"*Shhh, shhh, shhh. mon ami*, there are no waves here. There is no buzzing. It is still. *Hein?* It is quiet, oh so quiet. There is only quiet. *Shhh, shhh.* Hear the quiet? Hear the quiet."

His words soothed the Artist, whose breathing slowed and deepened. As if pulled upwards by a string, the suffering man raised his head.

Swollen from weeping, his nose and face were puffy and red; mucus dribbled down his chin. His eyes were a washed-out blue and struggled to focus. His shaggy head was bristled in red, sweaty spikes. He looked so utterly lost, almost childlike in his despair, that Luc reached for the edge of the sheet that hung over the edge of the nearby bed and gently tugged it forward to dab at the Artist's face.

The Artist reached out, grasped Luc's hands and the sheet, and rubbed his own face. This quickly turned to a brisk scrubbing, then a pounding.

Luc reached out his other hand to try and restrain him. "*Shhh, shhh.* No need, *mon ami.* No need. *Shhh.* Gently now. Gently."

Gradually, he was able to help the Artist to his feet and over to the bed. Guiding him with one hand and tugging at the sheets with the other, he was able to get him back into bed and tucked under first a sheet, then a woolen blanket, and then a quilt. The Artist still shivered, but his eyes were starting to focus. The blue in them clarified and then locked themselves on Luc's face.

"L—L—Luc? Where am I?" he managed to croak.

"You are in the establishment of Madame Bertrand, *mon ami*. This was meant to be an evening of pleasure and entertainment. Something appears ... not to have proceeded as expected." Luc chose his words carefully, weighing each one before letting it out.

The Artist looked around the room, his eyes widening. "I did this? *Non, non.*"

"Yes, *mon ami*. You did." Luc located the brandy bottle and two glasses, miraculously untouched. "Ah, I thought Mademoiselle Louise would have some." He began to rise, but the Artist grabbed his arm. "No worries, *mon ami*. I am here. I will get you some brandy. I think you need it."

The Artist let go and Luc swiftly crossed to the table, poured a small amount of brandy, and returned to the bed. "Now, sit up, *mon ami*. And sip. Sip slowly. Yes, that's it. That's it. You are looking more the thing," he lied, appalled at the state of his friend. "More the thing," he repeated. He took the now-empty glass to the table and came back. Propping up one of the other pillows, he warily settled himself down on the bed near the Artist.

"Luc, I did not intend ... I feared, but I did not intend."

"Of course you did not intend, *mon ami*. Of course you did not."

"It is just—" The Artist paused. "When I paint, you see, I hear, I feel, I see, and it passes through me and onto the canvas. But when I, when I ... see, hear, and feel, all that I see and hear and feel is trapped, and it is a storm, a fire, it is everything, and it carries me away. Yes, away, I am coming apart, burning up, every hair on my head, every hair on my body, each and every one. There is too ... there is too ... there is too much *life.*" He raised his eyes to his friend's face. "There is too much life. I do not know how else to describe it. I sound like an insane man. I have been treated as an insane man. I know this, you see." He searched Luc's face for understanding, a sliver of comprehension. "I know this, you see," he repeated.

Jean-Luc did not have the words, but he nodded. "You, you are an Artist," he finally said. "I am not. I do not, in the same way, but—"

The Artist reached out a hand and grasped his friend's. "There is a buzzing, you see. So much of the time. When I touch people, the buzzing grows louder. Louder and louder and louder." He stared at his friend's hand in amazement. "But I touch you and I feel silence, peace. With you, I feel peace. Why is that Luc?"

Luc could only shake his head.

"I must sleep," said the Artist. "Help me sleep, Luc." The Artist pulled Luc's hand and placed it over his heart. "Please help me sleep." He closed his eyes and within moments, began breathing quietly.

Luc attempted to settle himself on the bed, his hand uncomfortably grasped and trapped at an awkward angle. He felt the quiet thudding of the Artist's heart under his hand. Something had cracked, something had broken within the man in front of him, who conversely seemed even further away than ever before. It made Luc feel responsible for the man. He shook his head. He did not want this. The Artist was a living thing literally in his hands. The bones of the Artist's ribcage felt light and hollow, like those of a bird.

The fullness of the responsibility felt like a heavy curtain coming down. He almost gasped at the weight of it; it took his breath. It was all he could do not to jump away, off the bed. He had not asked for this, this thing. Even though he had returned home, he had still done his very damnedest to maintain his independence and the illusion that maybe, just maybe one day, he could set out again to see the world.

Yet here was this man, this stranger, wounded, damaged, who needed someone to look after him. Was there not anyone else? Must it be him? Surely the man had family, someone who cared, someone who could care for him. But as that thought arose and receded, it was replaced by another, of a tie between them, breastbone to breastbone, as if they were connected by a silken thread stronger than the coiled ropes of any ship. He realized that the hook went in long ago, when he and the Artist had quarreled next to that haystack. But now it grabbed and melted to his breastbone, as if soldering itself in place.

He found himself listening for the Artist's breath, waiting for the next heartbeat, terrified that one or both would suddenly stop. Each fresh breath, each reassuring reiteration of the rhythm under his hand, came as a relief. Though he wished desperately to pull away, he knew he was trapped more thoroughly than he had been trapped by anything before.

Eventually, he too slept and found himself on the deck of one of his last ships—was it the *Artemis?* He felt the breeze skipping towards him over the waves; the salt and the moisture of the sea filled his nostrils. He was alive, he was free, he was where he needed to be—he was home. He drowsily awoke when the Artist roused himself enough to say, "I hear your heart, Luc, I hear your heart." And then the Artist was asleep again.

Luc blearily looked at his own hand, his calloused, battered, and work-scarred hand, and marveled that it could bring quiet and peace to another human being. Then he too fell back asleep, back on his ship, knowing he was being carried away farther than he had ever been before. And for the first time in a long while, the ocean terrified him.

19 – The Hour before Dawn

Madame Bertrand saw them out herself in the chilly hour before dawn. She offered, without a word, an old but substantial woolen shawl for Luc to drape around the Artist's shoulders. She took them through the kitchen, using a candle to light the way, and as the two men stepped over the threshold, she laid a hand on Luc's shoulder. He stopped and turned to her. Speaking softly for his ears alone, she said, "Please know you are always welcome to my house, Monsieur Jean-Luc, but your friend, the Artist, he cannot return."

Luc dipped his head. "*Je comprends*, Madame Bertrand, *je comprends*." He let go of the Artist, pulled money from his pocket, and placed it in her hand. She looked down at it, nodded, and closed her hand into a fist. "*Bien.*" Then she kissed him on each cheek. "Go with God, young man. Go with God and be well." And with that, she turned and re-entered the house, closing and locking the door behind her.

Luc bent down to pick up his lantern. Pulling a box of matches from his pocket, he struck a spark and lit the wick. "Well, Monsieur Artiste," he said. "We have a light to see us home. You will have to walk, but you may lean on my arm should you feel weak."

Eyes averted, the Artist simply shook his head and took a step forward, clutching the shawl around his shoulders.

"Then we are off, my friend," said Luc. "Back home."

They moved much more slowly than they had on their way there the evening before. The Artist shivered from time to time, sometimes from the cold, and sometimes—it seemed—from reaction. But as the sun began to rise, accompanied by birdsong, he incrementally stood straighter and lifted his head. The colors of the dawn and retreat of evening shadows appeared to revive him.

He stopped to observe and said, "See how they move, Luc. See how it all moves, the sky." When they finally reached the outskirts of A–, he let out a sigh and briefly stopped again. "Home," he whispered.

When they reached Madame Sorel's, Gretchen stepped into the alley holding a jug of fresh water. The Artist wearily placed his hand on his friend's shoulder, as if seeking one final burst of strength, then let go, and slowly began to walk up the stairs to his room. He pulled the key on its round holder from his pocket and shakily tried to insert it into the lock. Once and then twice, but his hand jittered too much, and the key clanked against the lock, unable to fit itself. Gretchen abruptly set down her jug and rushed to the stairs, reaching them just as Luc did. The two stared at one another. Luc stepped back to watch silently as she darted up the stairs, took the key from the Artist, and putting her arm around his waist, helped him into his room and shut the door. Luc waited until she re-appeared.

"I will tell Madame that Monsieur Artiste is unwell," she said, and with that, she returned to the yard to retrieve her jug and re-entered the kitchen.

Luc stood in the alley, bewildered, dazed, and exhausted. His thoughts sluggishly slopped around his skull. His head hurt. His entire body hurt. He felt as if he had gone through some type of physical calamity. An earthquake, that was it. He had been in one once, in Naples, and he remembered the rumbling of the earth, the realization that nothing was solid, and that there was nothing to hold onto. Nothing. It had been like drowning on land.

Slowly, he made his way south. The ground underneath his tired feet seemed unstable, as though he were on the deck of a ship. The light breeze carried with it the tang of the sea, though he knew it could not be real. The urge to run, to leave, to escape scratched between his shoulder blades. He shook it off. He had chores to do, animals to tend to, before he too could collapse into his bed. But he was still aware of that silken cord and wondered how far it would let him travel before pulling him back. He could still feel the beating of the Artist's heart under his hand and wondered what he would do, if it stopped.

20 – The First Days Back

The Artist slept through that day, waking only briefly as the light slipped from bright to dark. He only ate a portion of the roll and cheese that Gretchen had surreptitiously carried up to his room and then he fell asleep again. He did not wake until the early fingers of dawn poked themselves through the open shutters.

He yawned and stretched. His body felt as it did after one of his attacks. What had he done? What had happened? He leapt out of bed and began searching through his jacket pocket. The bottle was still there, sealed and undisturbed, although Gretchen had carefully hung it up on one of the wall pegs. He sighed with relief and sank into the chair. What had he done?

He used the technique suggested by that last doctor: go to the beginning and work your way forward. And then he remembered—well, not all of it, but enough. He was with Mademoiselle Louise. His memory was a jumble of light, noise, heat, and an iron taste of fear in his mouth and then screaming—oh, God, the screaming was him. His head collapsed into his hands; his ears caught fire, and his face burned hot with shame. Screaming. And he had been doing so well.

But then, something new. In the midst of the chaos, a sudden harbor of quiet. A calm. A stillness which began at a tiny point then expanded outward, like the ripples of a stone thrown into a pond until it reached out and embraced him. What was that? And then he knew. It was Luc. Luc had touched him and the buzzing quieted and went away; the jangle of his thoughts had untangled themselves and flowed silently once again.

He stared at the memory in his head in wonder. No one was ever able to do that for him, ever. His mother tried, but the buzzing always spread to her own head, and the only mutual soother was his younger brother, placing a hand on each of their heads. But not even his brother had been able to do this.

In wonderment, the Artist stared at the memory, as though that circle of quiet was taking physical form in front of him. And then, he knew. He had to capture that, distill it, and transmit it to the canvas. Perhaps, in that way, the memory could help him again.

The buzzing resumed, but he was able to push it to one side. Going to the stack of blank canvases he pulled one out, along with his palette, the bag of paints, and a brush. He did not need a real-life model: he could see Luc clearly, as if he were in front of him. Almost feverishly, he began to paint.

After another hour, Gretchen knocked softly on the door and entered, but he ignored her, absorbed in his work. Skirting around him, she picked up the discarded bread and dried out cheese and took them out. She returned a short while later with some fresh bread and cheese, a small bowl of porridge, and a cup of coffee. She set all of this down on a chair and tiptoed out. Again, the Artist paid her no mind. He painted through lunch. He painted into the afternoon. Everything he thought, felt, knew, everything he had experienced that evening flowed onto the canvas and into the portrait that was emerging.

He was putting on the finishing touches when he heard a gasp behind him. It was Gretchen, coming to check on him again and retrieve the utensils from that morning to ensure they were returned before Madame Sorel realized they were missing.

The Artist whirled around at the sound, sending a fleck of paint flying off the end of his brush and landing on the floor. He bent to dab at it with his painting cloth.

"That is Monsieur Jean-Luc!" Gretchen said. "That is him, to the life. He seems so alive, as if he would step out of the painting at any moment. How did you do that, Monsieur Artiste? That is Monsieur Jean-Luc."

"Yes, it is, is it not? I wished to thank him for his care of me when I was ill. I wished to *capture* him, put him into the canvas, not simply on top of it. *Bah*, it is not dry yet, of course. But I must take this to him. My hat, Mademoiselle Gretchen? *Merci*. And my coat? No, no, it is no worry that I get paint on the sleeve. I am an Artist, yes? And now I must go. I must get this to Monsieur Luc."

Painting the portrait had not served as a total exorcism, but perhaps showing it to Luc would bring the quiet back, the stillness. Perhaps this time it might stay. He rushed out the door and down the stairs, running through the village fast enough to make him breathless, taking the road south until it drew closer to Luc's farm, and then cutting across the fields in search of him.

But he was not there when he reached the farmhouse. Looking around, the Artist could not see him in the surrounding fields either. Perhaps he was refusing to answer his door? The Artist knocked and knocked, until his knuckles were raw, but it was no good.

He thought about leaving the painting there, at the door. But if Luc had gone to another town, who knows how long he might be gone, and then it might get ruined! At that thought, the buzzing ratcheted up to a higher pitch. Suddenly dizzy, he put his hand on the door to steady himself and placed his forehead on the wood. His breathing slowed. "*Shhh, shhh*," he told himself, whispering in imitation of the voice that comforted him that night. "*Shhh, shhh*." He did not know how long he stood there, but his balance returned, and the buzzing receded. Picking up the painting, he retraced his steps to Madame Sorel's house and climbed the stairs. Suddenly, he felt hungry. Perhaps tonight he would go to the café and have a proper meal.

He carefully set the portrait down, but contrary to his usual practice, he propped it face forward. Staring at it, he reached into the pocket of his jacket. His hand searched through the notebook and pencils. It continued to dig until it encountered the bottle. His eyes still on the canvas, he pulled out the bottle, broke the seal, and took a drink.

* * *

92

Back at Luc's farm, the farmer slowly began to uncoil the tension that closed around him like the jaws of a trap when he heard the knocking. "Not tonight," he mumbled, "no, not tonight. I cannot face this. I cannot face *him*." He turned over again onto his side and fell asleep.

21 – Autumn and Winter

Days passed. Then weeks. The fiery golden colors of autumn arrived, flared, dimmed, and darkened to the stark contrasts of winter. The earth and trees were hard, sullen, and brown, etched against a wintry blue sky that was chilly, even as far south as the town of A–. The Artist presented his paintings of the Mayor's son; only the formal pose was accepted. He completed his single formal painting of the Mayor, which, too, was accepted. He received his final payment.

No more commissions appeared in the surrounding countryside. No money arrived from Paris or wherever his brother was travelling on his business, indicating that none of his paintings were finding a buyer. The level in the small bottle dropped and went dry. The Artist used some of his dwindling funds to purchase a refill. And then another. The *francs* and *sous* in his possession continued to decrease.

Madame Sorel and the other inhabitants of A– treated him as they always had. The only change was with Gretchen and Luc—the first presented a careful watchfulness, and the second retreated behind the wall of his seemingly standard bonhomie—but the Artist knew it was not the same between them. He continued to tramp the countryside, painting and painting and painting. The people and scenes he saw, the landscapes, all continued to travel into his Eye and out through his arm and hand onto the canvas.

But the buzzing became a near constant companion. The only times it went away, or he lost some awareness of it, were when he was painting or after he had taken a swallow from the bottle. At first, one swallow would quiet the sound for a few hours. Then it required two. And finally he was pulling out the bottle even while he was painting, without being completely aware he was doing it.

Then came the evening when he sat looking at just enough coins to see him through the next week. Reluctantly, stupidly, he stared at those thin pieces of metal lying in his palm. His shoulders slumped and when he stood, his head was woozy. He was failing. He had failed. It had all been useless. All.

He looked around the room. The portrait of Luc was still there, though now covered by a stack of more recent paintings. He went over and dug it out of the pile. It was the finest, the best, the most honest thing he had ever done. Somehow, he was able to put onto and into the canvas an almost naked rendition of another human being.

As he sat there, he was able to conjure up the feeling of that hand, resting on his heart, quieting the buzzing and the noise, bringing him back to center. Even through the fuzziness of the alcohol, he could still bring that forward, and a little piece of despair retreated. He opened his eyes again and blinked. He had done many self-portraits, and this was not one of them, but he understood that in capturing Luc, he also captured himself. He did not understand how or why—at least not yet. Sometimes understanding preceded his paintings, sometimes it appeared afterwards, and sometimes it did not appear at all.

Returning the painting to its place in the stack against the wall, he prepared to go down for dinner. He would ask Monsieur Capet to post the letter to his brother in the morning. Yes, that is what he would do.

* * *

The next morning, Gretchen stood at the sink in the large kitchen, furtively sneaking glances at the Artist while he ate his porridge and drank his coffee. Shadows were growing under his eyes; each day, the thumbprints darkened. He sat hunched over his food with his shoulder blades drawn together like two sharp wings. But where would he fly away to?

He rarely spoke to Gretchen anymore, only the occasional grunt. When she went up each day to clean his room, the chaos he left behind was increasing. He became careless with his artist's tools—brushes lay matted with paint for days, the spirit of turpentine left uncapped, flavoring the room with its acridity.

The Artist was going somewhere. She could feel it. But where? Or how? He looked increasingly insubstantial, and he returned from his day's painting and drawing excursions panting and limping.

A few days later, she found the portrait of Luc again. When lightly dusting the tops of the stacked canvases, they fell over, revealing the painting tucked behind. As she had the first time, she gasped and stepped back, struck anew by it. Then, she found herself pulled forward, mesmerized to the point of sitting down on the wooden floor to stare at it.

This time, she saw both men, the faces interchanging, though the features were clearly Luc's. How? She wondered whether it was some type of witchcraft or sorcery. Hesitantly, she reached out a finger to trace the jaw and lips. The texture of the paint and the canvas, which could still be felt underneath it, burned into her skin. Taking her gaze away from the painting to look at her finger, she blinked in surprise at its normal appearance, unmarked by its encounter. She returned her eyes to the portrait.

Monsieur Luc was there, fully present in front of her. As usually happened when she gazed at him, she felt something shift inside. She wanted to grab him, or have him grab her, and throw any of Madame's propriety out the window. But when she looked at the Artist, she thought of home and the dim echoes of her *Mutti*'s voice, and she knew she would follow him anywhere to get closer to those feelings.

When the light in the room changed, she leapt up, returned the canvases to their former order, and rushed down the stairs, praying against hope that Madame Sorel didn't notice her absence. Madame had not. But later that evening, Gretchen was scolded sharply on at least two occasions; she found herself clumsier than usual.

The morning after she had rediscovered the portrait of Luc, she opened her mouth to speak when he came down for breakfast. Her lips formed the words "stop" and then "stay," but she found she could not say them out loud. His closed-in body and the grey tightness that surrounded him choked them in her throat and locked her jaw shut.

He left without saying a word.

She tossed caution to the winds, sat down at his place, and let her fingers trace the edge of his plate. And then she put her head in her hands and began to cry.

She found herself saying, over and over, "Please don't leave me. Take me with you." It was only the sound of Madame's footsteps in the hall which propelled her upright and back to her chores.

22 – The Delivery

The Artist continued what had become his general routine—up early, breakfasting in the kitchen, a day spent sketching or painting, either outside or in his room, and evenings at the café. The only changes were the increasing distance between Luc and himself, and then, between himself and everyone else in the village. As the perceived distance grew, the buzzing expanded, filling his days, sometimes growing so loud as to block out the connection between himself and the object he was sketching or painting.

There was a constant gnawing question in his mind. Did the others in the village know of that night at Madame Bertrand's? He could tell himself repeatedly that Luc was his friend, Luc would not have said anything, but a creeping paranoia began to infect his daily interactions. He listened for the underside to a comment or looked for a sideways sliding of the eyes in all his contacts with others. The fever that had begun to consume him now was different from the energy of his paintings. This fever brought a flush to his cheek and a constant sheen of sweat to his face and down his back regardless of the temperature. The only thing that would numb the buzzing, along with his awareness of the sickly heat, was to take a pull from the bottle.

His painting began to suffer. A sheet of warped glass frequently dropped between his vision and the object he was trying to capture, distorting the movement he saw, twisting it into grotesque shapes. His hand would shake, and the pencil would skip on the paper, or the brush would stutter on the canvas. Finally, after an afternoon spent unsuccessfully sketching a self-portrait, he reached into himself to say: I must act. Which meant what? He turned from his reflection in the glass and looked into the gloom. Shadows were falling, and only one set of the shutters was partially open to let in enough light to sketch.

Luc. The painting the Artist had unsuccessfully delivered was facing a corner of the room. Like Luc, its back was to him. Luc.

He would reset things. He would take the painting to Luc at a time when he was sure—or as sure as he could be—that the farmer would be there. It would not be a public setting. No. But he needed to re-set, re-wind, re-something.

He barely slept that night and was up bleary-eyed before sunrise. He jumped out of bed, threw on his clothes, and carefully picked up the painting. He left his room and started down the stairs before Gretchen's light made its way to the kitchen. Heading south out of the town, his feet directed themselves to Luc's farm.

The wind picked up as he walked, so he kept a strong grip on the canvas. The air was cold and crisp, and his breath appeared before him like a faint cloud. To his left, the blue blush of early morning retreated as the orange and gold of the sun crept over the horizon. The air was crisply cold, but his hands began to sweat. Nerves, he told himself. Nerves. Nerves. His breath came in urgent puffs. As dawn fully broke, he found himself standing in front of the farmhouse door.

He lifted his fist, hesitated, and then brought it forcefully down. Once. Twice. Silence. He looked around him wildly. The buzzing picked up in his ears. The man had to be here somewhere! Then, around the corner, Jean-Luc appeared, his strong hands gripping two sturdy milk pails, and with Bruno at his heels.

The farmer slammed to a stop as if he had hit a wall. His face took on a wariness. A moment passed before he slowly moved forward "You are here early, Monsieur Artiste." His voice was rough and lacked its usual note of welcome.

The Artist swallowed. "*Oui*, I am, Jean-Luc. I have come to—I have something for you."

Luc spotted the canvas.

"Please."

Luc stared at him a moment longer and then nodded. "Very well, Monsieur Artiste. But I have chores to do. I do not have time for artistic things today."

"*Mais, non.* I do understand. I have not seen you of late when I have been sketching and painting. I know you are very busy. A farm has many demands." He realized he was babbling.

Luc grunted and opened the farmhouse door. "Come on, then."

The Artist followed him inside, shutting the door behind him. The farmer headed into the kitchen with his milk jugs and then returned to the living room and partially opened the shutters to let in the cold morning light. The hearth was still unlit, as sullen as the day. Luc did not offer the Artist a seat nor a cup of the coffee that was visibly steaming on the stove. He just stood there, arms crossed, to one side of the fireplace, waiting. Bruno placed himself at his master's feet, but did not settle. His head turned from one man to the other.

Grabbing the portrait in both hands, the Artist approached the mantel and placed it on top. Bruno growled slightly in the back of his throat, but he did not move. The light coming in through the semi-open shutters haloed the painting so that it seemed to glow. Luc's eyes widened and he took a sharp intake of breath.

"Do you like it then, Luc? Do you like it?" The Artist heard his words from far away. He was not used to begging or wheedling over his work. He hated the sound of desperation in his voice. It suddenly felt more important than anything he had ever done for this man to see and experience this painting, and to understand.

"What have you done?" Luc's question was a ragged whisper.

"What?"

"You are some kind of thief. You have stolen from me. You have stolen *me.*" Luc stepped closer to the hearth and the portrait with wide eyes. Abruptly he punched his chest, directly over his heart. "From here. You pulled something out from here."

"Then you see, Luc. You understand?" The Artist reached out, grabbing his friend's arm. "You see?"

Luc's gaze slowly moved down to where the two men were connected. His lips curled back from his teeth.

"Get your hand off me."

The Artist involuntarily took a step back, but did not break contact. "Get your hand off me. Devil! Thief!" Luc grabbed the Artist's hand and flung it away from his arm. "Is it not enough that you grab me, here!" He pounded at his heart again. Then, he punched the Artist over his own heart. "We are connected! From here to here!"

The Artist staggered back with the force of the blow.

"*Hein*?" Luc's face was crimson. "You have latched onto me. I tried to avoid this. I tried to avoid you. I cannot be responsible for you!"

"Responsible for me? No, that is not—"

"Yes, responsible for you! Needing to take care of you! And you are draining me. Is this what you have done to your brother? Is this why he stays away and never visits? I knew this and now I see it in your painting. You have taken some of me, stolen it, to put in your canvas. I did not give it to you. I did not give you permission! You stole it, and you are still stealing from me."

"No, no, Jean-Luc. You do not understand. I do not ask anything of you. I paint what I see and feel and hear. I transmit it and it flows through me onto the canvas. And so, I gift this to you. In thanks for our friendship."

"Friendship? What do you know about friendship? I am not some tree or sunflower, a crop you can prop up and use."

"Jean-Luc, what are you saying? You are no prop. I do not understand."

The response from the farmer was almost a howl. "And neither do I! I do not understand! I had made peace with my life here. But you have destroyed that. Every day, I walk my fields. I do my chores. I tend to my farm. And every day, I hear the sea. It pulls at me, trying to drag me away. And it comes ... it comes from you. You are pulling me into your world. You are making me a part of *you!* Where do you stop, and I start? The buzzing you spoke about? It has turned into the sound of the waves for me. The sea, it never leaves me. I hear it, I can taste the salt on my tongue. And this constant awareness is rubbing me raw. I cannot exist in your world." He sucked in his breath, as if to gather himself together. "This, this portrait. It is not decent!"

"Not decent?"

"It is not decent for a human being to be able to see so clearly into another human being—to lay that person bare in front of all the world. What are you doing to me?"

"Jean-Luc, I do not understand!"

The farmer's body sagged, as if this repeated denial by the other man had finally emptied him. Slowly, he lifted his eyes to the Artist's. "No, you do not understand. I see that now. I didn't want to. That you could see the way you do and yet not see anything at all—it is always the painting for you. Always and always, the painting alone. But it makes a pathway, here, and it goes in both directions." He paused, and his hand traced a loop between his chest and the Artist's. "But that seeing is not without effect, *mon ami*." The last was almost a whisper. "It forges connections where connections did not exist, perhaps should not exist." He paused again. "I have seen much of the world, more than most of the men and women of these parts. But I cannot understand this. I thought I might have been willing to throw it all aside and try, but no, I cannot."

He walked directly to the portrait as it sat above the hearth. Bruno shifted uneasily. Jean-Luc reached out a hand and traced the jaw. "And it is not just me, is it? It is somehow also you. How did you do that?"

He turned away from the mantel and looked at the Artist. The steel returned to his voice. "Take this painting out of my house. I do not wish to ever see it again. Go, before I forget myself. Just go." At that, he headed back into the kitchen and stood in front of the stone sink, hands gripping the edges so tightly that, even from this distance, the Artist saw that his knuckles were white.

The sound of the buzzing erupted like a swarm of furious bees, or a cloud of locusts. It took the Artist's breath away; it took almost everything away. Abruptly, he snatched the portrait and sprinted out of the house, only recovering once he was half-way back to A– and aware of his surroundings again. He realized the reason he could not see clearly was because tears were steadily spilling from his eyes until he was practically blinded. He came to a halt and used the back of his hand to dash them away.

He knew where he was. He knew exactly where he was. Yet he had never felt so lost in his life.

23 – Visitors from Paris

The days crept forward. At times the Artist felt like an automaton, one of those mechanical dolls he had seen once, exhibited in Paris. Other times, like a marionette, though he did not know who was holding his strings. Yet, somehow, he did what he always did—paint, draw, sketch. The circles under his eyes turned purple. His conversation, never ample, shrank further. He dimly noted the frowns and looks of worry from the residents of A– as he passed them either on the street or in the countryside. Claude-Joseph and his friend François ducked out of sight when he appeared, but he barely noticed. Jean-Luc infrequently stopped by Monsieur Capet's establishment and when he did, he and the Artist studiously avoided each other. He overheard the men placing wagers *sotto voce* on the cause of their falling out. But, as neither he nor Luc spoke of it, he believed the winnings remained uncollected.

And so, it continued until one day as spring was starting to emerge, the Artist returned from his painting to find a letter propped up on the chest of drawers. It did not look like his brother's hand, so he approached it warily. It carried the odor of Paris and his old life. He picked it up between his thumb and index finger, holding it away from his body, as if it were paper dynamite. His heart rate increased, and his breathing came in hiccup-y gulps.

He shook his head as if that would clear it, then brought the letter close to his face, and tore it open.

"Dear Monsieur Rouge," he read, *"Or, as our English compatriot Timothy would say, Monsieur le Ginger!* Bonjour! *You have been without our company for far too long—or is it meant to be the other way 'round? Well, I write with good news. We will be with you on the morning of the 12ᵗʰ; we plan to take the early train to arrive for a day of painting.* Jeunes filles *may be in attendance. No guarantees, mind*

you, but the countryside may offer enticements. Marcel successfully tracked down your brother for your location—the house of Madame Sorel, n'est-ce pas? We shall see you soon. We look forward to being treated to the best views and an excellent establishment (well, the closest approximate to such an establishment, being so far out in the wilds as you are) where we might relax in the evening. Will it be beer only? Pray God there is still a decent wine on hand.

> *Your comrade—*
> *Antoine"*

Oh, God, thought the Artist. Oh, God. His different worlds crashed together—he could not see his former compatriots here. He was no longer the same man; that man existed a century ago. But they would be here ... tomorrow. They will be here tomorrow. He fumbled in his pocket for the bottle. Recent funds from his brother allowed him to purchase a new one and there was plenty of liquid to take three deep gulps that burned from his mouth down to his stomach. Tomorrow.

He let the letter fall to the floor and looked around the room, which now had a crooked tilt to it. He stumbled to the door, flung it shut behind him, and bumbled his way down the stairs to the café. He ordered two additional glasses of wine with his dinner, causing the phlegmatic Capet to send his eyebrows to the top of his forehead, and the wobbly apprentice to view him with undisguised dismay and, perhaps, a grudging respect. He left the café without even the briefest of good nights, made his way home, and collapsed, fully clothed, on the bed.

The bright sunlight streaming through an abruptly opened door and an astonished, "Monsieur Artiste? Are you unwell? It is past ten of the clock!" from Gretchen finally roused him. His mouth tasted like what was that taste? He leaned over the bed and tried to spit out whatever it was that coated his tongue, but his mouth was so dry, nothing came out. This prompted another gasp from Gretchen and then a tut-tutting which bore a remarkable resemblance to that of Madame. He turned his head to watch her through his swimming vision. She bristled. Her figure wavered and sparked. With a groan, he turned his face back into the quilt.

"Monsieur! You must be up! This will never do! If Madame should see you this way, she will throw you out! What can be the matter with you? Must I duck you in the pump bucket!"

"*Non, non, m'mzelle. Non.* I will ... I will get up. Please lower your voice. My head is twice its normal size."

"It most certainly is not, Monsieur Artiste. It is completely its regular shape. But your face? *Peuh*! *That* may be twice its normal size. Up, up, up!"

Groaning further, the Artist pulled himself up and gingerly placed his feet on the floor, which appeared to undulate beneath him. Once standing, he extended his arms to maintain his balance and made his way over to the basin. A pair of surprisingly strong hands grabbed his head and forcibly dunked it once, then twice in the water. Gasping with surprise, he pulled free, scattering droplets everywhere.

"You. Must. Never. Do. That. Again," he wheezed to Gretchen.

"Hah!" She stamped her foot and strode out of the room.

* * *

She did feel secretly ashamed—to do such a thing was not correct, it was not proper—to enter the room of a man and to treat him this way! But she found a smile breaking out on her face, a small ember of her own authority and agency beginning to flare to life. She had done something; she had acted. And she had established a sense of ownership, right here and now, in that room and with that man.

She began to whistle one of Jean-Luc's sea shanties as she descended the stairs, the happiest she had felt in quite a long while. She was unsure where this optimism came from, but she didn't care. It was a beautiful day. And she had ducked the Artist's head in his wash basin and had roused him from whatever he was sleeping off.

She stopped, though, at the sound of a horse and cart pulling up in front of Madame's house, accompanied by a great deal of shouting and singing. What on earth? She interrupted her return to the kitchen and proceeded up the narrow alley to the street.

"Mademoiselle! We seek Monsieur Rouge! Is this the home of Madame Sorel?" A young man in a velvet suit, hat rakishly angled on his head, wielded an artist's brush as though some type of baton. He stood up in the bed of the cart, his friends grasping his legs to keep him upright.

"*Oui*, Monsieur." She stared at each of them in turn, attempting to take their measure. She suddenly felt protective of the Artist and that gave her a boldness she did not normally display with strangers. "And who might you be?"

The man scrambled off the back of the cart and swept a low bow. She counted: besides Monsieur Velvet Suit, there were additionally one, two, and, yes, a third young man sitting up front with the driver.

"We are a small company of artists from Paris," the man said. "I am Monsieur Antoine, this is Monsieur Marcel, that is Monsieur Timothy. He is English, pay him no mind. We keep him for entertainment. And this is Monsieur Geoffroi, which is a mouthful, so we call him Jules. Because we can, *n'est-ce pas*? We are here to spend a day painting picturesque country scenes with our esteemed compatriot who has made his home here. Monsieur Rouge! Monsieur le Ginger! Come down! We have arrived!"

During this very loud and emphatic introduction, doors and windows all along the main street had flown open. Even Madame Sorel had come to the front door of her house, to look with great displeasure at the men.

Gretchen watched Antoine gamble on Madame's identity, and then he swept into another low bow. "Madame Sorel! A million times *merci* for taking such good care of our *camarade*. We are here to remove him for the day, and we shall be taking our disreputable selves off as soon as we collect him."

The other men then joined Antoine in a chorus of "Ginger! Ginger!" until the Artist stepped out onto the tiny landing, his hat on his head and his jacket on his shoulders. This was followed by a great round of cheers and applause. As soon as he reached them, he was pushed up into the wagon, and the equipage took off. The show now being over, the spectators withdrew and shut their doors and windows. Madame caught Gretchen's eye and with a jerk of her head, sent the young woman scurrying back up to the yard and into the kitchen.

* * *

The Artist found himself heartily pounded on the back, while simultaneously being assaulted by a fusillade of questions. He put his hands to his head, which his friends immediately recognized as their common signal of too-much-to-drink-the-night-before, and they tempered their exuberance. Antoine spoke in a voice loud enough to be heard over the cart and horse but still as quiet as he could make it. "Did you not get my letter?"

"*Mais, oui,* I did, but I overslept and—"

"And who was that golden creature we spoke with?" interjected Marcel. "Might she be persuaded to accompany us, if we went back and asked nicely? For you see, we are without any *jeunes filles* today—they all have rejected our invitation for a day in the country."

"But we have brought a picnic!" exclaimed Jules. "And it is quite a handsome one at that. There is an inn near the railway station, and we enquired there as we wanted to fully experience a country picnic. We are not quite sure about the quality of the wine, however."

"You and your wine!" exclaimed Timothy. "But how are you feeling, my dear Ginger? You have had so many months to recover and never a word to any of us. We wanted to be sure you were still alive. Now, work before pleasure." Here, the other men groaned. "So direct us to the best spot to sketch and paint today. I want to capture something unique, something that is truly of this place."

The Artist peered around to see where they were on the road south. In a very short while, they would be approaching the edge of Jean-Luc's fields. His initial impulse was to shrink back and then he thought, no, why not. Let him see that I have friends, and Parisian friends at that. "Here, just here," he said, and pointed at the hill leading up to the trees. "While it is still cold, there is a fresh spring over that hill where we can have our lunch. And the top of the hill is the perfect spot for choosing a view."

"*Bien!*" exclaimed Antoine. The cart came to a stop, and the men clambered out, systematically disbursing their painting supplies and finally the picnic basket. Antoine had a quiet word with the carter, who nodded and then headed further south on the road. "He will come back for us at dusk," he declared. "Now, on to our painting."

Boisterous they may have been, but the men were serious once set to work. As hunger finally took each of them, they silently voted to take a break. They carried the picnic basket down to Jean-Luc's stream and ate and drank, regaling the Artist with their latest exploits and the gossip from Paris. At one point, far in the distance, the Artist thought he spotted Luc and Bruno, but he blinked, and the vision vanished. He might have imagined it. A short rest after eating, and then the men were back to their painting. The jingle of a harness announced the return of the carter, and they happily packed up their work for the day, cheerfully swapping their thoughts of what they had seen and captured and what they might yet do, should they have more time.

Through these hours, the Artist said relatively little and did only the briefest amount of sketching. His hand shook too much to capture anything, and the images jumped and danced before him; the energy was jangled and interrupted, almost angry. Finally, the lead broke and he could not find a replacement or a penknife in his pocket to sharpen it. This precipitated a feeling of such heaviness that he simply tucked the pencil away and let his head sink down upon his knees. He dozed until it was time to leave and then scrambled to his feet with greater steadiness than he had demonstrated earlier in the day.

Back in the cart, Marcel reached out to ruffle his hair. "Who is your barber, Monsieur Rouge? A bit ragged, if I do say so." The Artist gave a small smile and Marcel laughed. "Now," he continued, "should we repair to your fine dining establishment in A–?"

"Of course," said the Artist, feeling a twinge of unease. "The café, up there, on the left. That is where I usually have my dinner."

"Then that is where we will dine!" exclaimed Jules. Soon enough, they were pulling up to the door of the café and spilling down from the cart.

The door opened to the familiar heat, smoke, light, and noise that had become a second home to the Artist. All talk, however, stopped dead at the entrance of the group. Monsieur Capet looked up from his perch behind the bar and gazed questioningly at the men. Nervously clearing his throat, the Artist advanced and introduced his friends. "Messieurs, may I please introduce my fellow artists from Paris. These are Messieurs Antoine, Marcel, Jules ... *errm* ... Geoffroi, and Timothy."

The regulars looked suspiciously at the newcomers. Antoine stepped forward and swept off his cap. His suit and hat were the first of their type to be seen in A– and the men clearly were not quite sure what to make of them.

"Messieurs," Antoine said, "we are delighted to be welcomed to your charming town, and this esteemed establishment. My good man, your best table and your best four bottles of wine, *s'il vous plaît*. And a round of drinks for every other man here!"

The response was only a low mutter. The Artist watched his Parisian compatriots' faces fall; these were not the cheers they were expecting. Nevertheless, with a grim expression, Monsieur Capet nodded toward the Artist's usual table and one of the farmers at another table stood and provided his chair.

Monsieur Capet cleared his throat. "Do you have coin, Monsieur? I shall need to see it first."

"But of course! Will this suffice to bring us a hot meal and the wine?" Antoine held out some coins to the café owner who looked, counted them with a finger, and then grunted assent.

"Antoine, can you afford such largesse?" whispered the Artist.

"Don't you know?" interjected Timothy. "He has sold his first major painting. He has been treating us all quite richly this month—he even paid for today's train trip."

"*Oui*, it is true," Antoine said. "I have had my first good sale. So, I share it with my friends—and with my friend who has been gone far too long." He bestowed a warm and merry smile on the Artist.

The buzzing, regardless of the alcohol he had consumed over the past twenty-four hours, started up again. Sold a painting. Sold a painting. And Antoine had worked at his craft for not even half as long as the Artist. Jealousy. Despair. Failure. Desperation. All these emotions rolled over the Artist, and once the men were seated and served, he downed his first glass of wine practically in one gulp.

Monsieur Capet's food was good, hot, and filling, and the Parisian artists dined and enjoyed it. But the Artist left his food nearly untouched, focusing on filling up his glass and draining it repeatedly. The eyes of his neighbors appeared to be grilling him; he could feel reproach in them. As the night wore on, his friends talked happily, joked, and even sang, and it finally became too much for him. Abruptly, he climbed onto his chair and raised his nearly empty glass of wine.

It was more of a clamber than a climb. His footing was rocky. The two thimblefuls of liquid left in his glass nevertheless managed to slosh as his arm wobbled and wheeled. Droplets splashed on his already stained and frayed cuffs.

"Yes!" he shouted. "Look! Look! We are artists. These are my friends. We are all Parisians. I have shown them the countryside and they find it picturesque. They find you all picturesque. It is all terribly picturesque. The food, the wine, the views: they will have these memories to take back to Paris." The room grew quiet. The Parisians had stopped talking and were watching him, mouths agape. The men from A– seemed to have stopped breathing.

"So yes, picturesque. Quaint. Country bumpkins! I cannot wait to be gone. They have reminded me there is only one Paris, one place to be if one is an artist. So charming. Oh, so charming." Suddenly, he saw Luc, standing at the bar. He had not noticed his entrance and did not know how long he had been there. The Artist's mouth tightened; the buzzing in his head grew louder and he gave in to it.

"Yes, my real friends, true men of the world, men who *see* what an artist sees. No would-be world travelers here, who think they know so much of the world. To my friends!" He took the wine glass in his right hand, drew it up high over his head, and lost his balance.

Chair, man, and glass met the floor with a crash which seemed to reverberate around the silent café. The echoes of the shattered glass hung in the air.

The momentary tableau was broken by Monsieur Capet, who seemingly expanded to a monstrous size as he came around the bar. "Out!" His face was red, his cheeks quivering. "Out! Get. Out! You and your Paris vermin. Out!"

The Artist's friends helped him up and hurriedly dragged the dazed man into the night and onto the waiting wagon. He watched his four companions look worriedly at one another and speak in whispers, making uneasy glances at him. Antoine climbed up with the driver and directed him north, back to the railway town, and then paid him outside the inn nearest the station. The Artist said nothing. He was trapped in an echo chamber where he re-lived the moments, up on that chair, when he had shouted at the men of A— and then at Luc, and the look on Luc's face. And the look on Monsieur Capet's face. And the look on Monsieur Philippe's face.

He blindly followed his friends into the inn and continued to pour wine down his throat until a gentle hand on his arm stopped him, and his friends carefully helped him up to the room they had hired for the night. He dropped onto a pallet on the floor and fell asleep in an instant.

24 – An Unkind Cut

The Artist woke up late the next morning, alone in the hotel room. He was not entirely surprised that his friends left without waking him. He doubted that they could have. His head pounded. His ears were both ringing and stuffed with cotton. His thoughts were sluggish and unconnected.

He staggered to his feet, staggered out of the room, and groped his way down the stairs. "Hey!" yelled the innkeeper. "What time do you call this? You owe extra for delaying the cleaning of the room. I have a business to run. Pay!" A dull dread filled his stomach and climbed up to his throat. He wanted to retch but somehow did not. Reaching into his trousers' pocket, he found the last of his *sous*. He was a couple short, but the innkeeper took one look at his face and decided he had gotten the best of a bad bargain.

The Artist stumbled out the door and into the main square. The sun was far up, and the noises of horses, carts, shouts, and clangs brought him to his knees. The world swam and he buried his head in his arms, as if he were a bird cowering under a protective wing. A tap on his back was shortly followed by another. He raised his face to encounter that of the local gendarme, portly and frowning, nightstick at the ready. Somehow, he managed to scramble to a standing position, tottered forward, and then was thoroughly sick onto the stones of the road. Groaning, he attempted to bring himself upright once more. He wiped his mouth with the back of his hand. The sourness in his stomach was slightly better, a marginal improvement. The presence of the gendarme enabled him to find the strength to fully regain his footing and set off down the road in the direction of A–.

It was a nightmare journey. The road bucked and rolled in front and behind him as he lurched from one side to the other. The birds' calls were shrill and mocking. The sun beat down on his naked head—had he lost his farmer's straw hat?—as though it had fists, hitting him harder and harder. And the buzzing. The buzzing started out like a swarm of bees fleeing a coming storm. He wondered for a moment whether he was the storm, but realized the sound was coming towards him. Nearer and nearer. It began to drown out everything. As the tone slid higher and higher up the scale, the sky seemed to darken and pulse with thousands of their tiny, enraged bodies, until he fell to his knees in the road, his hands over his ears, shrieking in agony.

Abruptly it was gone, and everything stopped, as if he had stepped into that storm's eye, where everything was calm. He noticed the breeze was light that day; the recent cold snap had broken, and he could smell the soil and sense the seeds underground, ready to push through. The sky was so blue, so deep, the same, rich hues of the bottle.

The bottle!

His fingers frantically dug into the pocket of his coat. It was worth his life—where was it? Then his fingers closed around its short neck, and he pulled it up and out, holding it above his face so that the sun streamed through its milky glass, bathing everything in the blue. That blue. Precisely that blue.

He yanked at the stopper, opened his mouth, and tilted it.

One tiny drop fell, oh so slowly, and landed on his lower lip. He shook it, harder and harder, demanding more. It could not be empty. It could not.

His trembling fingers lost their grip, and the bottle flew, landing somewhere off the side of the road. He stared at it stupidly. What was he to do now?

And then he felt as if he were expanding. He seemed to be leaping across the kilometers to A–, and then to the other side of the village. He was seeking, searching, reaching. But as he huddled there on the hard-packed surface of the road, his spirit extended as far as it could go, he came up empty. Whatever it was, whatever could heal him, was too far away, gone, somehow unreachable. He snapped backwards, hurtling towards his body, only to be met by the enraged horde of bees. He clutched at his head again, trying to stuff his hands into his ears.

Somehow, he regained his footing. Somehow, he fled, running as fast as he could in the direction of A–.

He nearly collided with two short figures who appeared abruptly in his path. One part of his brain told him it was Claude-Joseph and François, but that knowledge felt too far away to grasp. He blindly pushed them out of his way and kept going.

The Artist was too out of breath to scream or shout by the time he reached the house of Madame Sorel. He grasped at the stair handrail, heaving and panting.

Somehow, he managed to climb the stairs. Somehow, he had not lost his key in the previous day's activities and this morning's pell-mell return. Somehow, he was able to fling open his door, rush to the basin, fill it from the ewer, and plunge his head into it. Grabbing a towel, he scrubbed and scrubbed. The buzzing continued. He re-plunged one ear and then the other into the water. He was frantic. Water flew around the room. He began scrubbing again.

The buzzing continued.

But now it was only one side of his head, located in one ear. One ear only. He stuffed a corner of the towel into the offending organ and the sound muted slightly. In desperation, he reached for his straight razor and brought it down, over and over again. The pain was acute and then it wasn't. Everything came into balance. His vision cleared. His breath slowed. The buzzing stopped. It stopped. Thank God for that. "*Mon Dieu, mon Dieu, merci!*" he whispered. "*Merci.*"

He patted at the wetness on his coat. The liquid was thick and heavy, seeping through his shirt. He took the towel and began to blot at it, trying to absorb the water. It should dry shortly. Then he could rest.

The towel in his hand grew wetter and heavier. Was he sweating? He pulled it up to dab at his forehead and froze. The towel, his shirt, were soaked in thick pools of dark red liquid. He looked around. Red droplets were scattered about him, as though he had taken a paint brush and shaken it all over the room. A waxy object lay on his right foot. He bent down to pick it up and found he was holding a human ear.

Something was wrong, something was very wrong. Holding both towel and ear, his bloodied hands pushed open the door and he staggered down the stairs, through the alley and around the yard, pushing through the hens as they clucked angrily. He pounded with his free hand on the kitchen door and almost fell through as Gretchen opened it. Madame Sorel stood behind her. Both women were covered in aprons, with the signs of baking on their hands and flour sprinkled throughout Gretchen's braid.

He handed the towel and the ear to the women. Gretchen screamed and did not stop, her mouth forming an "o" of horror. Madame Sorel's face drained of color, leaving her dark eyes and hair to stand out starkly in contrast.

"Please," he said, "please. I am better now. The bees are gone. Do not be afraid." And that was the last he knew for a long time.

25 – L'Hôpital

There were hours for the Artist when everything was blessedly still and quiet, and other moments when he was surrounded by a fog of gray and white. No ground under his feet, no trees or buildings, no people. He alternated between hanging there and walking, endlessly walking within the grayness, his body a memory. But to where or why or what never became clear.

There were snatches of sounds, smells, surfaces, and contacts in that fog. Occasionally, a bitter taste or a restriction of his arms. Once he thought he felt the hard wooden boards of a wagon, jouncing up and down. Another time, he smelled apples and then a harsh carbolic scent. A bird's song blended into the clanging of metal on metal. A great bell tolled somewhere. The scratchy coolness of linen sheets. Voices rising and falling. The pain receded. The sounds receded. Everything dissolved time and again into the gray and white mist.

Until the day he stepped out. A voice said, "It is time." A warm and feminine voice, a familiar tone.

"*Maman*?" he asked.

"*Mais non*, Monsieur. *Soeur* Félicité."

The Artist opened his eyes. He was sitting on a wooden bench outside a large, pleasant building that had once been—or perhaps still was—a house. It was chilly, but the first buds of spring were erupting from the branches over his head. Thick, fecund, and oh, so very much alive. He was wrapped in a sturdy wool blanket, and a straitjacket. His head was bandaged, one side tightly wrapped. The sounds around him were odd and muffled. He turned his head to see and hear the voice.

A middle-aged nursing sister was seated next to him, knitting needles and yarn in her hands, her scrubbed and faintly lined face framed by a wimple. He looked hard at the needles, and then again at her face.

"I am confident, Monsieur, that you are unable to harm either myself or yourself."

He twisted and tugged at the straitjacket.

"No, not quite yet, Monsieur. Perhaps today, once Dr. Henri has seen you." She leaned forward, peering first at one eye and then the other. "Perhaps you are truly back now. Dr. Henri has been gradually reducing the soporific as you have become less violent."

"Wh—" His lips did not want to come together to form the words. "Where am I?"

"You are at *L'Hôpital*. You do not remember. Yes, that is not surprising. You were out of your head when you arrived, alternately unconscious or shouting. Ah, but here comes Dr. Henri now. He will answer your questions. Dr. Henri, the patient has fully come 'round, as you predicted."

"*Bien, Bien*." A slim, dark-haired and dark-eyed man, with a thin mustache and a deftly shaped beard cut to a spade's point came into the Artist's line of vision. "It is good to see you fully awake and alert, Monsieur. It has been a while. You have worried your friends and your family."

"My brother, was he here?"

"*Mais, oui*, Monsieur. He arranged to have you brought to *L'Hôpital* from A–. He has come to see how you are doing."

"He brought me here?"

"Oh, no. That was a farmer from A–. *Pardon*, I do not recollect his name. He brought you on his wagon. It was the fastest way to get you here, with the least inconvenience, though you did sustain some additional minor contusions from the journey. The farmer was most concerned, most concerned. I will send word back to your brother, and to A–, that you have improved."

So, Luc had been the one to bring him. Despite his actions and his memory of the days and weeks prior to whatever had brought him there—that part was still covered in the grayish fog—his friend forgave him. Perhaps Luc—and the villagers—had not deserted him either. Maybe he was not, then, totally cast out. The slenderest thread of redemption appeared, and he grabbed onto it. I cannot let this go, he thought.

The Artist looked back at the doctor. "How long have I been here?"

"A fortnight, Monsieur, recovering from the combination of the infection from the attack to your head, and the after-effects of such potent alcohol. Your brother reports you were forbidden from drinking anything stronger than a single glass of wine. But it appears you have been breaking that stricture. It does not do well with your system, which becomes over-excited."

"The buzzing. It stops the buzzing."

"The buzzing. I see. You have been playing physician then. Sometimes, such attempts can be a worse cure than the original ailment, Monsieur. I think we can let your limbs free for a little while." The doctor glanced over his shoulder and beckoned to two orderlies. With a careful look at the Artist, and without breaking eye contact, he reached out to the buckles holding the straitjacket in place. "We will try this very slowly, Monsieur. Georges and Jacques will assist. Do not be afraid."

The Artist numbly nodded his head, letting the three men remove him from the jacket which was pinning his arms to his body. He shivered at the sudden cold. *Soeur* Félicité stepped forward to settle the blanket firmly once again around his shoulders.

The doctor pursed his lips, running his fingers over his beard. "We will see how you do, Monsieur. A while longer in the fresh air, with gradual walks, eggs, and cream, should lead you back to your full health."

"My notebook, Doctor? And may I paint?"

"One thing at a time, Monsieur. I do not wish for you to get over-excited or over-heated. No." He held up a hand. "Do not fear. Your notebook and pencils are not far. The farmer from A   was most insistent you would be lost without them. Everything is in my office for safekeeping. We will see how you do through the rest of today and this evening."

The doctor took a step back. "I must go on with my rounds. You are making excellent progress, Monsieur, simply excellent. *Soeur* Félicité will be here, with Georges and Jacques nearby. Take some time to sit quietly. Then you will need to go inside for dinner and medicine. *Au revoir.*"

He strode across the path, onto the circular drive before the building and through the double front doors. *Soeur* Félicité seated herself again and resumed her knitting.

The Artist closed his eyes and listened, extending himself as he had not been able to do since that horrible day on the road, which was coming back to him in bits and pieces. The sun on his face held a tinge of warmth, but it was the light he drank in. The breeze tucked itself around his head, trying to work its way under the blanket, which he clutched more tightly around himself in response.

He felt the calm, centered presence of the nursing sister at his side. He heard a bee exploring the flowers behind him. If he listened closely, he could hear the breathing of the two hulking orderlies nearby. Yes, he could still feel the ever-present energy; it had not left him. This gave him confidence that soon he would be able to pick up his pencil, and then his paints.

Taking a deep breath, he screwed up his face, seeking the buzzing. Was it there? Was he being pursued? Nothing. Just the sounds and the breeze. He was safe. For now, he was safe.

He brought his hand up to touch the bandage which was wrapped around one half of his head. He was tentative, light in his exploration. For once, tender with himself. What had he done? He could not remember. The fog refused to retreat when he probed where he thought the memory should be. Physically, there was only a dull ache.

"*Achh*, Do not fiddle with your wound, Monsieur," admonished the nursing sister.

"I will be careful, *Soeur* Félicité. But I do not remember. What is this? Did I fall? Was I in an accident? Did someone attack me?"

She set her knitting down in her lap and directed a measuring look his way. There was compassion in that gaze, but no pity.

"You do not remember, Monsieur?"

"No, I have no memory at all. Will I be able to remove these bandages soon? They chafe, and they restrict my hearing and my vision."

"They will be removed tomorrow and cleaned. If Dr. Henri agrees, we will allow you to observe the wound in a looking glass. It became badly infected, and the resulting fever was a worry, very dangerous. But it is healing quickly."

The steadiness of her gaze held him. Foreboding settled deep in his belly, but he managed to keep the fear at bay. For the moment.

"You will always be marked, Monsieur," she said gently. "You will not be able to escape this. Some actions cannot be undone."

"Some actions? What actions?"

"Your ear, Monsieur."

"What about my ear?"

"It is gone."

"Gone?"

"*Oui.*"

"But, how?"

"You truly do not recall?"

"No!" He almost exploded with impatience. Her response was a clamping together of her lips, but she did not draw back. He felt, rather than saw, the two orderlies step closer. "*Pardon, Soeur* Félicité. But I truly do not know."

"You cut off your ear, Monsieur." She shook her head, and now the pity surfaced in her eyes. "Your ear is gone."

26 – Brother and Sister

Madame Sorel had not seen her brother in weeks. She had walked out to the farm; Gretchen had walked out to the farm. Each took gifts of food in a large wicker basket: rolls or other tempting favorites fresh out of the oven and retaining enough warmth to entice the most finicky palate, but there had been no response at his door.

Today, she was not taking silence for an answer. Today, Madame Sorel dressed up in her Sunday best and borrowed the trap from Monsieur Adam. At her feet rested not only that day's wicker basket, but also what was previously simply a painted canvas, now enclosed within a simple, yet elegant frame.

By the time the Artist was carried away to get help, all those days ago, it was late in the evening, and she had reluctantly but firmly locked the door to his room and stumbled to her own, exhausted by what she witnessed.

But Madame's need for order and tidiness could only be held back so long. The irritation in her mind grew louder and woke her earlier than usual the next day. She surprised Gretchen while the young woman was still preparing the kitchen for the morning's meal. The girl had jumped back and slopped the water she was getting ready to set on the stove. Madame Sorel had a moment of something—compassion, solidarity, comradeship—or merely the connection of two people who had gone through an appalling event together. She lightly touched the maid's arm and spoke gently. "Today, we clean. And I will accompany you."

It was Gretchen who brought up the rear of their small procession, carrying the rough sponges and bucket full of soapy water along with a broom tucked under her armpit, dragging behind her on the stairs. Madame led, a full apron covering her dress, holding her copy of the key. Their progress up the stairs was deliberate but slow, and they halted in front of the door. Madame took a deep breath, inserted the key, and turned it. The door swung open.

Chaos greeted them—canvases messily piled, open shutters, and a fine coating of dust over everything. A jacket and hat lay on the floor. Torn shirts and trousers spilled out of the wardrobe. A trail of blood was smeared from the basin to the door. And it was so cold, so cold. The women shivered, though Madame was able to bring herself quickly under control. Gretchen continued to shake, faintly but distinctly, as she set the water bucket down with a thump.

Madame tutted as the suds cascaded over the edge. "Be careful, girl!" She waved her arm. "Begin sweeping. I shall deal with the rest."

Without further conversation, the women began to clean. As she worked, silent tears spilled down Gretchen's cheeks. When her nose began to run in earnest, Madame tutted again and handed her a handkerchief from the pocket of her apron. It was a hitherto unknown kindness—at least, one she had not indulged in for many years. "Really, I am growing soft," scoffed Madame to herself. But she retained a memory of a small girl, shaking with a fever in her tiny attic room, and Madame hushing her and bathing her forehead with a rag dipped in cool water. She shook her head and continued tidying.

Over the next three hours, the room began to reassemble itself. Madame took down the battered case from the high wardrobe shelf, carefully folded the Artist's clothes, and tucked them inside. Unsure of where it should be sent, she placed it back on the floor of the wardrobe. She directed Gretchen to take the scattered brushes down to the pump and clean them with the turpentine and water for good measure before placing them back in the Artist's canvas bag. The bed was stripped and remade. Every surface was dusted, scrubbed, and polished. The canvases were the last pieces, carefully stacked against the wall, their backs to the room.

While Gretchen was down at the pump, Madame noticed the portrait of Luc. As she carefully dusted the tops and sides of the canvases, the sheer number of paintings piqued her curiosity. She'd had no idea there were so many! Portraits of the countryside of A–, people, sky, Paris, and other places she imagined the Artist had been. They were most unusual, not in the typical style of what she would deem as art. Nevertheless, something in them called her. It was almost as if she could slip inside, as though the paintings were alive. "*Bah*, ridiculous!" she declared out loud. Nevertheless, as she continued to flip through them, she could almost feel the breeze on her face, hear the breathing of the sitters, imagine the tick of a clock in a room, taste the sunlight.

She gave another firm shake to her head and sought to stand up and let them be. But the portrait of Luc caught and held her. She almost forgot to breathe. It could not be anyone else. It was Luc, alive in a way she had never quite seen him—at least, not as an adult. Her brother: the boy who chased a dog around the farm, who hung from the apple trees in the grove, who set off to see the world with a jaunty cap on his head, leaving a painful lump in her throat. And then the harder and more self-contained man who returned but whose touch was gentle during those first days when she tried to make sense of a world in which she felt completely alone as a new widow. Her hand went reflexively to her mouth, to hold in the cry which rushed from her lungs and up her throat. She had never seen a person's soul captured, in all its three dimensionality, on a thin bit of rough canvas. Her hand left her mouth to reach out and touch her brother's cheek.

It wasn't even a thought, really. It was an act of impulse, of the moment, and yet she had never been surer of anything in her life. She snatched up the canvas, rushed out the door and down the stairs. Doing her best to shield the canvas from Gretchen with her body, she waved at her and exclaimed there was something she needed to do. Then Madame fled out the alley, down the street, and to the workshop of Monsieur Philippe.

She arrived out of breath, wearing her apron, with her hair in messy wisps around her face. Monsieur Philippe and his two apprentices were startled by the out-of-character whirlwind that burst into the workshop. Quickly, occasionally gulping down a breath, Madame informed

Monsieur Philippe of her wish for a simple yet elegant frame of the finest workmanship. And she wanted it quickly. Monsieur Philippe bobbed his head and agreed.

And now, several weeks later, it was finally done. The painting was with her in the buggy, wrapped in brown paper and tied with a string. She reached the farmhouse and clucked at the horse to stop, with just enough pressure on the reins to indicate that she meant it.

Madame Sorel carefully dismounted, retrieved her bundles, and marched to the front door. No hesitation or else she might lose her nerve. She set down the painting and knocked. Silence. She knocked again. Silence still. And then she began to pound, yelling and sobbing at Luc to open, in the name of God, to open the door that instant.

That last assault did the trick. The door opened to a disheveled Luc, hair long and shaggy, deep circles under his eyes, his mouth open in dismay. Madame Sorel further astonished them both by hurtling herself into her brother's arms and clinging to him. "Thank God! Thank God! *Mon Dieu!*" she said. Gradually, the shock wore off, and Luc responded, wrapping his arms around his older sister. They stood on the threshold, rocking back and forth, before Madame pulled away, dabbed at her eyes with her fingertips, and—resuming a few shards of her regular imperiousness—directed her brother to pick up her bundles. Wordlessly, Luc did so.

The interior of the farmhouse was dark and dusty; the shutters were closed, and the smell of stale sweat and pain filled the front room. Madame strode over to open the shutters and throw up the sash on each window. The brisk air began to blow through.

"This will never do," Madame said.

"I know, sister, I know."

"I shall send Gretchen to you tomorrow. You cannot live like this, Jean-Luc."

"I know," he said again.

Madame stood in the lessening gloom, looking at her brother as if seeing him for the first time. The man who stood in front of her with eyes cast downward was thinner than he had been. His cheeks were hollow, and his shirt was dirty with food stains. While he had never been a particularly fastidious man, he had always taken care of his appearance.

"What has become of you?" she asked.

He shrugged.

"*Hmph.*" She took the basket into the kitchen and set it on the sturdy table. "Tomorrow!" she declared and stepped back into the front room.

Luc nodded.

"*Bien.*" This time she headed back to the wrapped portrait and picked it up. "Here, this is for you."

Luc's eyes widened as he grasped the wrapped edges. He set it on a chair and began to unwrap it. As the portrait emerged from the brown paper, he breathed in sharply. The portrait fell against the back of the seat.

"I do not want it," he said. "I told him so before. I do not want it."

His sister stepped forward and took his face in her hands. "*Mon petit,*" she said, an endearment she had not used since he was the tiniest of little boys. "You must. This is you. This is yours. He would want you to have it. He painted it for *you.*"

"*Non*! How could I? What if he should die? What if we were too late? What if—"

"What ifs buy nothing in the marketplace, Jean-Luc," she said sharply. And then, with an old softness. "It is yours. It. Is. Yours. And it is time for you to take ownership. I will send Gretchen to you tomorrow."

And then she turned and left, shutting the door firmly on her now weeping brother. Her hands were shaking, and she felt tired all over, as if she had just walked for miles. It took three tries to climb back into the trap. Eventually, she did, and the world began to regain its normal axis. She pulled a handkerchief from her reticule and dabbed at her eyes and nose. She patted the front of her hair, ensuring all was well, and then reached back to check that her bonnet was securely positioned on her head.

Clucking at the horse, she turned it around and returned to A–. For the first time—since the day of the blood and the screams, after several days of watching the Artist twist and turn in a fever, after waiting for some direction from his brother in Paris as to what to do, and then making a bed in the back of the wagon, after watching her brother's strained face as he insisted on driving it to the hospital in the faraway town—Madame Sorel felt a tingle of hope and a lightness in her hands as they grasped the reins.

As she drove, she sensed the beginnings of spring. It was as if she could feel something stirring under the hard-packed earth, the leafless trees, even in the blue of the sky. Impulsively, she stuck out her tongue to taste the air and laughed at her own foolishness. There was the hint of sweetness there, she would almost swear to it. Still laughing, she tapped the reins to keep the horse moving forward. She felt like she had just been released from the winter.

Her thoughts moved forward in a lighter vein. Perhaps she did not need to rent out the room right away. Perhaps she could leave it for a bit. There would be no harm in that. It was still winter. Later in the spring would be time enough to advertise. For now, the Artist could retain his place in A–. And she would have her brother back.

"I think you are recovering well, Monsieur Artiste."

The Artist raised his head. He could hear the term now without the buzzing starting up, the sensation that he was under attack gone. He could hear the name again as a term of respect, and not of derision. He knew it meant he was getting better and soon would be able to leave.

Dr. Henri stepped fully into the Artist's small room. A narrow cot—with severely tucked in corners, covered by a warm and practical woolen blanket—lay along one wall. In front of the open window were an easel and a canvas. Various completed canvases were stacked against the opposite side of the room. He had begun painting again, and the speed and urgency of the endeavor returned, though this time without the underlying mania threatening to erupt.

The two men's eyes met, and the Artist set down his brush. "May I?" requested the doctor, with a slight diffidence the Artist found gratifying.

"*Bien sûr*," he replied.

Dr. Henri approached the canvas, looking over the Artist's shoulder. He remained silent and then he took a deep breath and released it. "Last night was beautiful, to be sure. As your physician, I must first ask, did you take any rest at all?"

The Artist shook his head. "I could not," he finally managed.

"I can see that. What you have done here—it is so alive. The sky moves. The stars are spinning. It is a thing of glory. Truly, is this what you see?"

"Truly, yes. It is what I feel when I sit or stand and look. I do not see only with my eyes but with all my senses, even with my skin. I listen. I taste. And then the world passes through me and onto the canvas. At least, that is what my goal remains. I wish the transmission to be as pure as possible. I am a means, an expression of what I am seeing. For example, the night sky."

"Yes. Yes. As your doctor, I must remind you to continue to practice the need for containment. For setting up walls. Yes, yes, I know you aspire to, *need* to, remain open. I do not wish to disturb that. It is as vital to you as breathing, you have told me so. But you must act like a valve—do not let it overwhelm you. If you become overwhelmed, you will not be able to function in the way you desire. We are but human vessels, Monsieur Artiste, and we have our limits. And if we acknowledge those limits, well, then, perhaps that makes us—conversely—limitless?"

"Dr. Henri, you are a philosopher. I am but a man who slaps paint on a canvas or scribbles a pencil across a page. But I will do my best to obey your adages and prescriptions." The Artist swallowed. Each hair on his head stood a little straighter with the strain of what he was holding in. So, he released it. "When may I leave?" He watched the doctor's face closely, searching for a hint, a direction, a sign. The only response he received was a measured look, but no indication of the doctor's thoughts.

"You feel you are ready to leave, Monsieur Artiste?"

"*Mais, oui*, Dr. Henri. I have made great progress. The buzzing is gone—the bees no longer swarm me. I can paint again. I do not feel the urge to numb myself with drink. Ants no longer crawl over me so I must wriggle and writhe. I am cured, or as cured as I will ever be. I am ready, Dr. Henri, to return to my life."

"And where would that life be, Monsieur Artiste?"

"Eventually, for my career, I know I must travel to Paris. But, for a while, I would like to return to A–. If that is at all possible."

Dr. Henri turned around, searching for the room's second chair, partner to the one the Artist used for his painting. He seated himself and pulled two pieces of paper from his pocket.

"I have written, Monsieur Artiste, to your brother in Paris. I have also made enquiries in A–. And I have received responses."

Dr. Henri unfolded one of the letters. "This is from your brother. He is happy to welcome you into his home in Paris, for as long as you desire. I do not think it good that you live on your own the way you used to, so this would be a possible choice, with your family and people you love nearby—though I understand your brother must travel for his business. And Paris is Paris—not the most restful of environments for recovering and rebuilding one's life."

He stopped, folded up this paper, and unfolded the other. "This is from your former landlady, Madame Sorel. She has stored your belongings, and her room is still available to you, at the same rates and terms as prior. In her letter, she offers to keep an eye on you. She states her servant girl is also available to assist, and that you have friends in the town. Obviously, A– would be quieter, though it is also where you fell ill."

The Artist nodded. His lips pressed together. His blue eyes began to fill, and he wiped away the tears with the back of his hand. The tears were more frequent these days. Dr. Henri said it was part of his recovery and that his emotions would settle more in time.

The Artist found his voice, initially husky, but he was able to speak after clearing his throat. "I am grateful, Dr. Henri, so very grateful. My behavior was such—I did not think my brother would wish me near him, nor that Madame Sorel and my friends in A– would want me within a kilometer of the village."

The doctor folded up the second paper. "I should add that your brother has set aside funds for you to travel to Paris, or to A–. If you travel to A–, he will, at least for the meantime, provide you with the means for your room, board, and supplies until you are truly back on your feet." He looked directly at the Artist. "Monsieur, the choice is yours. If you are ready to spread your wings, the door is open, not just—" He smiled and gestured. "Not just the window."

The Artist lifted a hand to scrub through his hair. He turned away from the doctor and looked at his painting. He knew what he wished to do.

"I will return to A–," he said, still looking at the painting. Then he turned to face the doctor. "I will return to A– and see if they honestly will still have me. If not, I shall go to Paris or perhaps another place, maybe this time by the sea? But I will come to that when I come to that." He stood, as did the doctor. "*Merci,* Dr. Henri."

Dr. Henri's dark eyes warmed, and then faded, the momentary concern quickly snuffed out and covered with his usual inscrutability. "*Bien*, then it will be a trip to A– we shall need to plan. I shall write to your brother, and to Madame Sorel, to let them know. We shall make arrangements." He took a moment, as if weighing his words. "I have valued having you as a patient, Monsieur. I believe *L'Hôpital* and my treatment have done you some good. Our paths may not cross again, but I will know your paintings anywhere. Make sure to take some rest." He turned and left the room.

The Artist watched him leave, and then took his seat again, his legs suddenly trembling. Freedom was terrifying and joyful. He was happy, an odd feeling. Joy was something he picked up from the world around him and recognized as it passed through him onto the canvas, but it was not something that normally came from within.

A memory swam to the surface—sitting with his brother in his father's study on a Sunday, while his father read a passage from a book of sermons. The actual spoken words had flowed over him at the time. He thought they had missed him altogether. Instead, he had only paid attention to the music of those words rising and falling in his father's harsh, nasal voice, and the ray of light working its way across the desk. The room had felt suffocating, like a prison cell. It was as if his father and his father's world occupied a different reality, a different universe to the one in which he himself wished to live. The only means of escape were focusing on the music and the light and the energy of the life he could sense around him. But he was never allowed to escape for long.

The end result was a sense of always being apart, always at fault, always a failure. The recollections of being called out for his stubbornness, his willfulness. The sense of always searching for something while having his hands tied behind his back and being pushed down to occupy a smaller space. The sense ... his thoughts skittered to a stop. And in that instant, the walls lifted, and he saw those constraints were simply gone.

"*Ah,*" he said out loud, "so this is grace." Because in that moment, the world he had tried to serve, a world he had never been indifferent to but which he had believed indifferent to *him*, had turned and touched him briefly and lovingly on the scar where his ear once was, before resuming its passage.

28 – A Return to A–

It was summer again, and the Artist was finally released from his latest captivity. He carried the tiniest of bags with a change of clothes—a gift from his brother—along with cheese, sausage, and a sturdy chunk of bread wrapped in a piece of waxed paper tucked into the pocket of his new coat.

He was still weak. This was the longest distance he walked since leaving the hospital, but he'd insisted he must do this on his own. He took the train a few stops and got off at the proper station, and then walked by himself back to A–. Dr. Henri had shaken his head at this proposed excursion but ended up agreeing. The excitement on the Artist's face was not the fevered energy which had plagued him during those early days of recovery, but merely—merely—the anticipation of going *home.*

No one in A– knew he was returning that day. If he had sent a letter ahead with his arrival particulars, someone might have come to fetch him, but he wanted the time to absorb the familiar sights, sounds, and smells. The dusty road. The ripe trees. The fields brilliantly full. The birds darting about, feeding their growing chicks. He wanted to feel the countryside and let it feed him.

Miracle of miracles, he had a place to come back to in A–. Madame Sorel maintained his room at no additional cost. He knew it was waiting for him. Her letter had starchily added the offer was not open-ended and that she hoped to see him within the fortnight, but no later than six weeks from the date of the letter.

Then his brother had written to him that two—*two!*—of the Artist's paintings were sold back in his hometown to an old school friend who was an up-and-coming outstanding citizen. The man wanted to show his sophistication by displaying modern art on the walls of his parlor and had already provided payment. It was not much—those paintings had sold for a song—but he gladly instructed his brother which of the two paintings held in his care he was to send.

And the Artist was drawing again. He was painting again.

And now he was going home.

He approached the outskirts of A– almost too soon. He nodded at a few of the townsfolk along the way. Claude-Joseph and his friend were not in evidence, so he assumed they were safely tucked up in the classroom today. No Monsieur Philippe. No matter, he would see them tomorrow. Monsieur Capet's café sat placidly in the late morning sunlight. The front door stood open with the young woman half-heartedly sweeping the stoop. Her jaw dropped at the arrival of the Artist. She forgot her dignity enough to let go of the broom and race back inside, yelling Monsieur Capet's name. Then the Artist was being enthusiastically pounded on the back by the café owner, with anxious looks in between each pounding. "You will be back here tonight, *hein*? There will be many who will wish to see you, Monsieur Artiste. You gave us quite the fright!"

The Artist found himself grinning with a smile wide enough to crack his face in two, and even getting in a couple of poundings of his own on Monsieur Capet's back. Promising he would, indeed, be there that evening, he picked up his small case which was dropped in the road by the force of the welcome and walked the remaining meters to the home of Madame Sorel.

Once again, he found himself standing in front of the house with the blue shutters. An eerie feeling, almost of *déjà vu*, passed through him—a sensation that he had been swept by a fast-moving river from that day long ago to this. He knocked.

The door opened to Gretchen's astonished face. "Monsieur Artiste! It is you! We did not expect you! We are not, oh, one minute." And then she was running back into the house, the door left open, while he heard her calling, "Madame! Madame! Monsieur L'Artiste has returned. *Il est ici*!"

"Half a moment, girl. I am coming. Do not shout—we are not a tavern." And out of the dimness of the interior hallway, Madame Sorel came into view.

She looked as she always looked: the good bourgeois housewife, all in order, her baking apron covering the front of her dress. She halted on the front step and looked him up and down, her piercing blue eyes seeming to see everything. "So, you have returned, Monsieur Artiste." It was a statement, not a question.

"*Oui*, Madame."

"*Hmph*, about time as well. I could not hold your room forever, you know. A great deal of demand from Paris, as you might guess. I continue to have parties interested in hiring it."

"*Oui*, Madame."

"*Bien.* Well, you are here now. That is good." She turned away. "Gretchen, fetch the key for Monsieur Artiste. We retrieved your key from you—" She halted, and something looked as if it might break free but was quickly contained. "We retrieved your key before you left us, and we have held it for your return. Gretchen! Where is that wretched girl?"

"Here, Madame. Monsieur, here is your key. I did not know you were coming, so the ewer is not filled. I shall take care of it shortly, Monsieur."

"That is all right, Mademoiselle. Thank you for your troubles. I shall set my satchel up in my room and take a short walk."

Madame Sorel's eyes narrowed. "Monsieur, you are lately risen from your sickbed. If you overexert yourself, you will end up back in it. And nursing services are not included in the weekly fee."

The Artist smiled. "*Mais, non,* Madame. I will take care. I am glad to be back. And it is a fine day, a fine day. Tomorrow it may rain, then I shall rest. But today, I wish to be outside."

"Very well, Monsieur Artiste. Here is the key. Gretchen, hand him the key. We will see you in the kitchen tomorrow morning at breakfast. I wish you a good day, Monsieur. A good day."

"Oh, and Madame, I expect delivery of some canvases from *L'Hôpital*. They should arrive within the week."

"Very well, Monsieur Artiste." With that, she turned on her heel and re-entered the house.

Gretchen lingered for a while, frankly appraising the Artist. He could see she studied him as if she were trying to use that picture of him to rub out another, one that he could not see himself, but which he could tell distressed her.

"I am not going anywhere, Gretchen," he finally said.

"Welcome back to A–, Monsieur Artiste," she responded, dropping her head briefly before pulling it back up with a quiet smile. "Welcome home."

"It is good to be home. It is good."

Key in hand, he headed up the alley and the stairs, unlocked the door, and pushed it open. His room, *his* room, was just as he remembered, as he had painted it. He felt the room curl around him, questioning, interested, curious, waiting. "I am home, Room. I have returned. It is time to do some painting, Room. Yes, some painting." He looked at the canvases stacked against the far wall, their backs to him. "But not today. Not today."

Setting his small bag inside the wardrobe, on top of the packed bag of his things that had sat there for all those weeks, he left the room again and headed out.

Without hesitation, he went south. He followed that familiar pathway, feeling the sun on his face, breathing in the scents of the trees and the flowers, and took the remembered turn to walk towards the farm. Summer was in full spate and some of the early crops ready for harvesting, so chances were he would not find his friend at home. He felt compelled to try, regardless. From the moment he learned Luc had brought him to *L'Hôpital*, he held onto a glimmer of hope for their friendship. The reception by Monsieur Capet, by Gretchen, and even by Madame Sorel had strengthened that further. But this was the final test, to tell him whether he was truly home.

He walked up to the front step. Tidy rows of flowers flanked each side of the door. It looked more domesticated than it had the last time he was there. He wondered what that meant. He knocked.

The door opened. Jean-Luc stood, looking at the Artist in momentary astonishment, then reached out to engulf the slightly framed man in a bear hug. "Monsieur Artiste! You have returned! You live to stroll the countryside again!"

The Artist further astonished himself by breaking into a laugh, "Monsieur Luc! I have indeed returned!"

"But we did not know of your coming. Why did you not tell someone? I would have fetched you."

The Artist shook his head. "I wished to do this journey on my own. I wished to walk and absorb. I wished to feel the sun on my face. I wished to *feel* A–."

His friend shook his head but did not question further. With a broad sweep of his arm, he beckoned the Artist to enter. "Come in, come in! Smoke a pipe with me! It will do your lungs good! I have some new beer. And apples. And even," a wry glance, "a new hat. Come in! Come in!"

The Artist stepped into the room, a room which had become darkened and fused in his memory with recollections of despair and rejection. But these memories would not adhere to the sunny and comfortable sitting room of today. Jugs of flowers sat on the small table and to one side of the mantel; the windows were open, and a light breeze teased its way through. Luc's dog lifted up its head from the hearth and woofed a welcome. And then he saw it.

There, in the middle of the mantel. The portrait. Now it was enclosed in a solidly carved frame that was polished until the wood shone. It appeared to glow and give off warmth, and it sat there as if it had always done so. It was the heart of the room. The Artist let out a grateful sigh. All was well. He was home.

Luc busied himself in the kitchen, then brought out beer and food on solid farmhouse plates. "Sit! Sit!" The two men sat in front of the hearth, munching and drinking, in companionable silence. Luc jumped up to take their empty dishes back to the kitchen, and then got down his pipe and an extra one from the pipe rack next to the fireplace.

"You have taken up the pipe, Luc?"

"*Mais, oui*. I am a proper gentleman of the countryside now, a proper squire, and so I must smoke a pipe. My sister offers me the services of Gretchen two mornings a week to help keep the farmhouse less like a bachelor's den. I am becoming a good *bourgeois*."

"Never, my friend, never!" And the two men laughed. The remainder of the afternoon passed in comfortable spurts of conversation, punctuated by silence. As evening fell, Luc noticed the Artist's energy was flagging, and so he hitched up the team to the wagon and drove them both into town to share a meal at the café. Before they left the farmhouse, however, Luc passed him a rough straw hat, a replacement for the one he had lost during those terrible weeks before. And two fresh apples.

Yes, he was home.

29 – A Day Out Painting in A–

That day, the Artist waited until the sun was fully up to set out with his easel, canvas, and paints, so he got a later start than he liked. He decided the light was just right at this time of year at the edge of the small forest that lapped one border of the town to the north. He went most often to the south, into the open fields, to watch the men and women while they planted and later harvested. He had just one more building to pass before he was free of the town's boundaries.

A small breeze tugged at the brim of his rough, straw hat, and he looked up as he reached to pull it back down. His eye was caught by the upstairs window. In it, two young boys were standing and watching him. He recognized them. The son of Monsieur le Maire, Claude-Joseph, and his best friend. What was the other boy's name? He could never quite recall it.

He released the hold on his hat and lifted his hand in a greeting. The two boys watched him and then, without much change of expression, waved their hands in response. He noticed, however, that their focus was on something they were holding. He squinted to see if he could catch a clearer glimpse. Ah, a black handle. A tapered and silver muzzle. The boys were of an age; they were going to be taught how to shoot.

He turned his attention back to the road before him and the escape promised by the trees. His Eye had already selected a spot with two trees growing together in a way that drew him, as if by a magnet. He was eager to get out his paints to follow the line of trunks as they both pulled together and apart, fused and held themselves separate. He knew when he focused, with the light falling just so, he would see that the brown of their barks was in fact many different colors and textures.

It was the discovery of the colors that gave him the most joy. The unexpected flashes of a particular hue which surprisingly found a home amongst the others. And it was not only colors but movement—solid objects were never still but fields of motion. He could not understand why others did not see this and, in the spirit of being truthful to his vision, he was not afraid to paint that movement.

And then he was there, at the spot he dreamt of the night before, which he was relieved and, at the same time, unsurprised to find existed. Some mornings, both image and location were clear, and he set off to reach them as quickly as possible. Sometimes, it was only the image his mind conjured, and he would spend a day or even days wandering in search of its mate. The fact that others might consider his visions strange or even uncanny did not trouble him in the least. It was the way things were, and he accepted it.

He set his bag down, opened and steadied the easel, propped up the canvas, and set to work.

He painted steadily through the day, pausing only briefly to eat the baguette and plain country cheese his landlady grudgingly provided. No apples today; perhaps tomorrow. He was thirsty but expected to pry a cup of something from the café on his way home.

The light was fading now, and soon it would be too dark to paint. He took a last regretful look at the two trees and began to pack up his gear. He carefully wiped the brushes on an old rag and wrapped them up tightly in that same rag before placing them back in his sack. He had some turpentine in his room, in which he would soak them when he returned. The easel was stuck, as usual, so he had to give it an extra tug to collapse it back into itself. The paint was drying well on his canvas, but he picked it up gingerly, taking care not to smudge any of the remaining wet spots. Encumbered once again, he turned and retraced his steps to the village.

As he crossed the boundary between town and countryside, he heard the slightest whistle by his ear. Such a small thing, nothing that could mean anything. Curious, he paused. It was not an insect. No, something bigger and heavier. Suddenly, he felt a weight in his head, as though it had abruptly ballooned and gained in density from the moment before. In the next moment, his head was the lightest feather, merely tethered to his neck.

He stumbled briefly, and then righted himself. His thoughts were momentarily confused but began to reform. There had been a sound before the whistle. He looked up, following the memory of the sound, and encountered the window he had noticed earlier that day. The window where the two boys had been standing.

They were there again now, tall leaning against short, although this time their mouths were frozen open. He saw the taller of the two—was his name Jean? Or Joseph?—holding the pistol. The window was open. And he saw that the pistol was pointed. Out. And down.

For a brief moment, the two boys were replaced in his vision with his brother and himself, standing at an upstairs window with one of their father's pistols, which they had pilfered from his drawer. They were using it to practice shooting at a blackbird that was perched on the tree outside their bedroom. He remembered himself firing. He watched the black feathers expand in a last attempt at flight, and then it was down on the ground. He stared and stared at the still heap of bird, there on the ground. There on the ground, where he was standing now. Though his feathers were red, not black.

And then he knew. Those two boys were not himself and his brother. But they might have been. He watched one drop of blood fall near his feet. And then another. These boys—they were children with their whole lives ahead of them. He did not wish to frighten them. No, he would return to his room and stop the bleeding in the basin there.

That was the refrain running through his mind as he lifted one of his laden arms in a wave of greeting. He saw the two figures relax, relieved all was well. Nothing had happened. They would not be found out, and life would go on as before.

The Artist continued his walk through the dusty streets of the village, a slight hesitancy or tug in his step the only sign anything was out of the ordinary. No one noticed as he made the short remaining way to his landlady's house and slowly climbed the outside stairs to his room. It was just another evening. No one saw a thing. Not for a long time.

30 – Death of an Artist

Monsieur Capet and the others noted the Artist had not appeared for his evening meal at the café. He occasionally missed an evening, but was always back the following night. They simply assumed he was engaged in "one of those artistic moods that overcome men of that sort," or so stated the apprentice who usually held up the wall in a seemingly drunken stupor, surprising the other men present at how much he was taking in as he leaned there.

It was Gretchen who observed something was wrong. When the Artist did not appear for breakfast, she climbed the stairs to his room with Madame Sorel's spare key in her hand. "Monsieur? Monsieur Artiste? Are you there?" She knocked and heard only silence, "Monsieur, are you well?"

There was no response. She began to insert the key into the lock, but the door swung open at that slight touch. The room was dark, the shutters still firmly closed. It took a minute for her eyes to adjust from the bright morning sunlight. The darkened shapes in the room, from the closest to the door, began to take on clearer definition. The first thing she noticed was the Artist's bag, easel, and canvas. After his return from *L'Hôpital*, he became much more ordered with his things, and she grew used to seeing his canvases neatly stacked, and his brushes thoroughly rinsed and drying. Instead, the bag was dropped on the floor inside the doorway, its contents spilling out. The easel was nearby. Yesterday's canvas was also on the floor, face down. With a cry, she darted towards it and turned it over gently. The paint had been largely dry when it fell; any smudges the Artist would be able to fix.

But where was he?

And then she heard the sound, not quite human. The breathing was ragged and almost like a rattle. It sounded like a beast, a monster, there in the shadows. She hastily crossed herself as her hair stood up on her neck. Looking wildly around, she prepared to flee. But there was no accompanying movement, and she froze in mid-dash. "You are not a child, Gretchen," she whispered. "You are not a child. You do not run."

Peering deeper into the gloomy room, her eyes made a circuit of the space and stopped at the bed. In the dim light, the coverlet looked darker than it usually did, which struck her as odd, and a dark mass lay on top. Taking a step closer, she could barely make out that it was the Artist who lay there, curled into a ball, barely moving. He was still fully clothed, down to his muddy boots.

With a cry, she ran to the shutters and clumsily opened them, allowing light to flood in. But then, seeing him, momentarily paralyzed her again. Her mouth worked to find words, but none came. This was worse than the last time. Much worse. She cautiously approached where his head was and bent down. A choking sound escaped her own throat as she realized he was the source of that horrible sound, which now seemed unnaturally loud in the room. Each breath dragged like a rake over a stone floor, scraping and pausing and scraping again. The coverlet was darkened because it was soaked with blood.

And then she saw it, the small bullet hole, round and blackened on the edges, stark against his pale face and his bristly red hair. But where was the gun? She grabbed hold of the idea and held on, a cause and effect that made sense in her tumbling thoughts: If she could find the gun, perhaps he would be safe, perhaps it would never have happened. But she could not see it anywhere, at least nowhere obvious, and fear suddenly gave her feet wings. She ran down the stairs, across the yard, into the kitchen and down the hall.

"Madame! Madame! You must come! Monsieur Artiste!"

Madame Sorel looked up crossly from her embroidery. "Good heavens, girl. Have I taught you nothing? You must not run around screaming and shouting to bring the house down. What has the man done now?"

"Oh, Madame, I cannot say. You must come. I think he may be, he may be—" The rest of her words tumbled into sobs.

Alarmed, Madame Sorel got to her feet and headed through the house and out the kitchen door. "I thought he was cured," she muttered under her breath. "That doctor promised me. This is the last time. I have a respectable home. None of these goings on can continue. He must leave. This is the—" She paused as she reached the top of the stairs and hovered on the threshold. Time stopped. But she forcefully restarted it by stepping into the room and taking in the mess and the bed.

"*Mon Dieu, mon Dieu,*" she whispered, crossing herself in an echo of her servant. As Gretchen had, she approached the bed and bent down. She heard his ragged breathing, a harsh rattle. The wound had crusted and congealed, but he had lost so much blood.

"Gretchen! Gretchen!" She turned and saw that Gretchen had followed her up the stairs, but remained on the threshold, hands to mouth, shaking. "Gretchen, go to Monsieur Philippe at once. Have him drive for the physician and bring up my basket of medicines. And then fetch Monsieur Capet."

Grateful to have something concrete to do, Gretchen turned and ran down the stairs.

"Oh, Monsieur Artiste. What have you done? Why have you done this?" Madame repeated.

It seemed an age, but then Gretchen returned with the basket. "Wait, girl. Before you fetch Monsieur Capet, let us put this room somewhat to rights, then I will begin tending to Monsieur Artiste and you can fetch help."

Mutely, Gretchen carried the ewer and the cloth to the bedside. Madame Sorel began to dab the blood. The Artist moaned softly, but barely stirred.

"*Non,* this is bad," Madame muttered under her breath. "Help me, Gretchen."

Together, the women gently maneuvered the bloody coverlet off the bed. The blood had soaked through to the sheets beneath. "I will need your assistance to undress him and place him in some clean nightclothes. Then we can try to make the bed around him. It is not proper, Gretchen, for you to do this, but I need your help. I cannot do this alone, and we must have him ready by the time the doctor arrives."

"*Oui*, Madame."

Quickly, and in concert, the two women stripped him of his shoes and muddy clothes. Gretchen grabbed his nightshirt off the knob on the wall and they pulled it over him. Madame tutted slightly at the blood which smeared on her bodice, but then clamped her lips shut and continued working, somehow managing to remake the bed from freshly laundered sheets set on top of the wardrobe just two days before. Her hands were brisk and efficient but gentle, and she cradled his head against her breasts while she directed Gretchen on how to maneuver the bedclothes.

"Take these downstairs and place them in a bucket of cold water, girl, then fetch Monsieur Capet."

"And Monsieur Jean-Luc?"

"There will be time for that later. Now, go."

Gretchen fled the room, carrying the ruined clothes wrapped in the blood-soaked coverlet and sheets. Madame Sorel looked down at the Artist again; the wound had begun to ooze. "Oh, my poor young man, what have you done?" She went to fetch the chair, set it by the bed, and gently began to sponge at his temple again, then wiped at his face.

"Where is the doctor? And what will I tell Luc?"

* * *

Since he returned to his room, the Artist's existence had become a grayness, broken by a series of flashes. There was darkness, pain, and then a drifting away. Then a flash, like lightning, the sound of footsteps, a gasp, and then he became aware of the light on the other side of his eyelids. He groaned slightly. He wanted the darkness back. The darkness was soft. He could drift away in the darkness. The darkness carried him, cocooned him, wrapped him in safety.

And then there were running footsteps again. And silence.

The lightning again. Madame Sorel. He felt himself lifted and moved. He felt coolness from the cloth. His head was on fire, but the gentle pressure soothed him. His heart began to beat harder, trying to respond to the movement, noise, and the presence of other people.

Cool sheets.

The sunlight was less harsh. Dimmed. Softer light. Candles?

A man's voice; wide hands with tapered fingers and an authoritative touch. "Can you hear me, Monsieur Artiste? Can you hear me? Answer me, *s'il vous plait.*"

The Artist raised his hand to bat away the probing fingers.

"Who did this, Monsieur Artiste? Who shot you?" Madame's voice. Imperious, commanding.

He struggled to hold onto the thread. The boys. The room. These people. The boys. There was something he had to do. To say. It was very faint now, but he had to hold onto that task a while longer.

"I did," he whispered.

"What?"

"*Moi,*" he put all the force he could manage into that response. He hoped he had been heard. But the effort caused him to begin panting, and he could not try again.

And now he is by himself in a warm, dark space. A light flares, as if the covering on a lantern is being raised to illuminate a scene that appears for a moment, and then fades abruptly once again to black.

The lantern shows a man plowing. A light breeze ruffles his black curls. He stops. Silence. The sea is gone. The salt tang has left his nostrils. He shakes his head as if to clear it. He looks bewildered, even bereft. He put his hand on his chest. Again, silence. He rubs at a pain—the snapping of a cord. He stands still a moment longer. Then he drops the plow and begins running, a golden dog at his heels.

The lantern shutters, then the cover is lifted again: a dark head and a carefully manicured beard. "*Non,* what did I miss? I thought he was cured, at least for a while longer. Oh, *pauvre* Monsieur Artiste. What did I miss?"

The blackness returns, and then the lantern flares: Paris. A telegram. A matching head of reddish hair, a body which folds itself down to the floor and begins to rock back and forth. "*Non, non, non.*"

Then the lantern flares and he is standing in front of a familiar door. It is a door to a place from childhood both feared and anticipated. It begins to open, and this time the Artist knows there will be no judgement behind it. So, it is done then. A pool of sunlight spills through the doorway, liquid gold pouring across the floor at his feet, the yellows and golds and whites swirling in patterns he has never been able to capture. His breath catches. He takes one step. And then another.

And finally, there is no separation between what he is seeing, feeling, and hearing, and what he intends to convey to the stretched cloth. Now he is becoming the vision itself, the living canvas. He feels the energy move through him—it embraces him, holds him up, and it does not overwhelm. And it—*she*—does not terrorize. Instead, she smiles and gently caresses his cheek. *My love,* she says. Or is he the one saying it to her? He laughs and bounces the apple up and down in his hand, bringing it to his mouth, and taking a bite.

31 – What Came After

As Jean-Luc skidded to a stop in front of the farmhouse door, Bruno nearly collided with him. Madame Sorel stood on the stoop watching, Monsieur Adam's pony and trap were nearby. The farmer's hand began to shake, but he pushed open the door and she followed him in. Both stopped once inside and stared at each other.

"He is dead, Jean-Luc. Monsieur Artiste is dead."

He stared at her, his lips moving soundlessly.

To fill that painful silence, she spoke again. "What was he to you?" Madame Sorel's words appeared to echo in the room. "What was he to you, brother, that you take on so?"

"Just a man, just a man." He rubbed a spot on his breastbone, then stared in astonishment at his hand, as if he expected it to look other than it appeared. He shook his head. "What did you say happened?"

"He is gone. The Artist, he shot himself. He has died."

Luc backed up until he was practically in the cold ashes of the fireplace. "What?"

"It is sad, terribly sad, a tragedy. We do not usually see such things here, in A–. But he was an artist, not one of us. His time with us was always going to be short. Our lives can go back to the way they were before he came."

"Wait, what? He is dead? Can I see him?"

"A telegram was sent to his brother and the body has been shipped to Paris. He is gone."

In point of fact, the telegram was not yet sent, the body not yet taken away. The Artist still lay in his bed, the sheet pulled over his face, a rosary laid on his head to ensure the state of his soul. Madame Sorel knew it was a sin to lie, but she thought this was more a deflection of the truth. He was not gone yet, but he would be soon.

"You did not tell me? You did not call me?"

"You were busy. You were working in the fields."

Her brother continued to stand there. Then he turned and looked at the portrait. She was not sure if he was seeing it. His eyes appeared— what was the word she was searching for? Her own head felt suddenly fuzzy. Ah, yes, blind. He appeared as a blind man.

She started again, trying to draw him back into the room. "He would always have left, my brother." She looked at his slumped shoulders. "You belong *here*, Jean-Luc. In A–. With me, your only family. And this farm. It is not an easy life, but it is a good one."

"He was my friend." Luc turned around, his eyes burning into hers. "He was my bosom friend. Of all I have seen and done in the world—" His voice trailed off. "He was my friend. Perhaps I might—if I had known in time—"

She interrupted him. "It would have made no difference, brother. When he was found, he was already dying. The doctor could do nothing. He had lost too much blood."

Her tongue formed the words again, as if it were passing back and forth over a sore tooth. "What was he to you, brother, that you take on so?"

Jean-Luc moved as if his limbs were under water. He drew out a pocketknife from his trousers and used the tip of the blade to gently run along the image's cheek. His other hand touched his own cheek, as if in some sort of reverse mirror. His face, and not his face.

He began to speak: "He was just a man." The knife lifted and then, as if held by an automaton's mechanism, it plunged into the portrait and dragged itself down and out, slicing the painting from top to bottom.

"He was just a man," and the knife plunged again.

Madame Sorel stood frozen in horror. He seemed to her a sleepwalker, but one she was terrified of awakening.

And then he plucked the painting from the mantel, the canvas hanging in shreds, and dashed it to the floor, the frame shattering with the force of impact. The violence, the crash, then the silence. Luc dropped the knife, turned, and walked into his bedroom. Bruno howled and launched himself at the closed door but received no response.

As though she had been released from whatever had gripped her brother, Madame Sorel fell to her knees. She swallowed convulsively and, finally, she began to sob. For what she did not know. It was a purely visceral reaction to the scene she had witnessed and the events of the past hours. She rocked back and forth, hugging her body on the cold flagstones. She was not sure whether her brother could hear her or not, but he did not emerge.

Finally, her breathing began to settle, and she struggled back to her feet. She pulled a handkerchief from her sleeve and buried her face in it, trying to return to some semblance of normality so she might leave and find her way home. The broken painting and the knife remained on the floor. Stooping, she retrieved the blade and placed it carefully on the mantel. She took the detached pieces of the broken frame and tossed them into the fireplace. The shredded canvas was the last thing she retrieved. She was ready to toss it into the fireplace as well and light it on her way out when something stopped her.

Perhaps not now. Perhaps not yet. A wild idea crossed her mind: I am a seamstress; I can heal this.

Heal this? What was she talking about? Her lips began to tremble again, and she struggled to bring them under control. Before she stepped outside, she carefully wrapped the shredded canvas into a scroll of sorts and tucked it under her arm.

32 – A Landlady's Duties

The telegram arrived, as expected, announcing the visit of the Artist's Businessman Brother the following Monday. Madame Sorel invited him in to share a dish of tea as he waited for the final packing and removal to be done.

There was a resemblance between the two brothers: red hair, beard, slight frames. But there, the likeness ended. This man's hair and dress were neatly cut and fashioned. His quiet demeanor was that of a successful businessman: self-contained, orderly, organized. Madame Sorel searched his face for more of a connection to his brother and found it in his eyes. They were gentle. While perhaps they did not see as far as the Artist's, she felt a sudden comfort in their familiarity. There was a slight shake in his hand as he picked up his tea to take a sip. She watched him fight to regain composure and succeed. So, a stranger, but not completely.

"And who else might have paintings created by my brother in A–?"

"Truth to tell, most people. You should stop by Monsieur Philippe's woodworking shop and at the café—I know the Artist did some paintings for Monsieur Capet. And Monsieur le Maire has some as well. We all knew him, your brother. He was … he had become a fixture in the village. Most people had a sketch done by him or a small painting of some sort. My brother—" She abruptly broke off and took a sip of her tea. Really, this would not do. She could feel a wobble make its way into her voice. She attempted to clear her suddenly constricted throat.

"Your brother?" prompted her visitor.

"My brother knew him." She plunged forward, her thoughts beginning to race. *Oh, where is that girl?* "Forgive me, Monsieur, but I am training a new maid, and it is early days. My previous housekeeper, a fine young woman, just began keeping house for my brother. My brother is a bachelor, you see, and his house was in a terrible state. What is a good sister to do? But his gain is my loss. Pardon, as I was saying, my brother knew yours, as all the others in the village did."

Really, where was this garrulity coming from? The thought of any silence in this room, with this man, suddenly felt dangerous, as if something might slip, though she didn't know what that could be.

"Anyway," she continued, "the others are carefully stored in his room, as you saw, the ones, that is, which he did not give, trade, or sell to people in the village."

A pause. The Brother cleared his throat. "And the gun? Has the gun been found?"

Another pause as Madame took a sip of her tea and then carefully returned the cup to its saucer. "No, Monsieur, the gun was never found. It remains—" She pressed her lips closed and took a careful breath. "It remains a mystery. He hid it well. How he made it upstairs after—" She shook her head.

The Brother slowly nodded. The conversation was at an end. He rose, gave her a formal bow, and left.

That evening, Madame Sorel sat in front of her parlor fire, and carefully unrolled the slashed canvas she kept covered in her large workbasket. Delicately, she picked up her needle and, with tiny stitches as invisible as she could make them, she continued where she had left off. One day Luc would want it back, and it would be waiting. She had done what she could for her brother for now, and she could have this for the future.

The Artist was gone. Her brother was still here and would be settled with Gretchen. The girl would look after him; nature would take its course. If they were to have children, well, then Jean-Luc would most definitely remain close. And life would continue as it had before in A—. It was time to put an advertisement in the Paris papers again. Though perhaps for holidaymakers or travelling businessmen. A more secure income. Artists, those like her previous lodger, were far too disruptive.

She ran a proper house. Her standards were high and would remain so. Yes, that is what she would do.

She looked at the flames in the fireplace. She loved watching them. There were so many colors and hues, moving and shifting, a field of motion. They warmed and comforted her, and she did not feel quite so alone. It was then that she felt it, the tiniest of touches. The house with the blue shutters wrapped its arms around her. She relaxed in its embrace. No, she was not alone.

Acknowledgements

They say that writing is a solitary pursuit, but when I was finally able to carve out time in my life to do what I had always wanted to do, I found it to be a community—of both readers and writers.

When they say it takes a village, that doesn't apply just to childhood. I have been fortunate beyond words to have been surrounded, my entire life, with an incomparable village of amazing humans from all walks of life and from all over the world. I will not be able to name you all. Nevertheless, please know each of you carved a permanent place in my heart, and I am incredibly grateful for you.

First of all, thanks to Mary Vensel White and the Type Eighteen Books team for believing in this novel and working so hard to get it out into the world. I am incredibly grateful.

To the participants in the 2017 Writing the Waves Workshop, who heard the original draft of what I thought would be a short story, thank you. And to all the members of the Virtual Writing Group whose keen eyes and quick ears continue to make my writing better with each session, thank you.

A special shout out to fellow writer Chris W. Higgins, who leant his legal background to helping me with the business bits at the end—thank you.

To the people who, over the years, gave me words of support which have kept me going in spite of the long wait to bring this book to the world: to Susan Oliver in Seoul, whose English class birthed the Wise Family Classics known as "The Wail of a Banshee" and "The Diving Suit"; to Vicky Herrera in Manila, who told me—"You are a writer"; to the late and much missed Couze Venn in London, who said on my first tutorial with him for my M.A., "Well, you can write"; and to poet Juan Delgado here in California, who told me, "You need to write."

To all my beta readers, who took the time to read and give me your thoughts, thank you. If I leave anyone off, my sincere apologies, but they include: the Ladies Night Out Book Group (who decided to read an earlier manuscript version of the novel for their bimonthly book pick), John Biddick, Norie De La Cruz, Jade Valour, Lisa Lynne Lewis (for reading it *twice*), Victoria McLaughlin Scott, Dc Lozano, and finally to my Barkada of IS Manila sisters who are there for me every day.

To the wonderful librarians at A.K. Smiley Public Library, who have been so incredibly supportive. I especially want to thank Monica, Shannon, and Julia.

To the memory of my poet grandmother, Ruby Robinson Wise.

To a wonderful fellow writer and supporter, my brother Dr. J. Macgregor Wise.

To my parents, John and Donna Wise: How I wish you were still here to see that a book I wrote has finally made it into the world. You remain with me always.

And to my best and first reader and editor on any writing project, my cousin, the amazing playwright and screenwriter C.S. Whitcomb—thank you, Cindy, and much love.

About the Author

After an international childhood lived throughout Asia because of her father's aid work, Tracy Wise has spent her career in theatre, opera, and then higher education administration. She currently writes university presidential speeches, campus communications, and news stories in California's Inland Empire. She has a B.A. in Theatre and Spanish from Washington University in St. Louis (which includes a year at the University of East Anglia in Norwich, U.K.) and an M.A. in Cultural Studies (a historiography degree) from the University of East London in the U.K. A life-long passionate reader, she designs social media for the Friends of the Redlands, California A.K. Smiley Public Library in her free time.